The Little Book of the 1960s

Dee Gordon

The History Press

First published 2012

An exclusive edition for The Works
Midpoint Park, Minworth, Sutton Coldfield, B76 1RN

The History Press
The Mill, Brimscombe Port
Stroud, Gloucestershire, GL5 2QG
www.thehistorypress.co.uk

British Library Cataloguing in Publication Data.
A catalogue record for this book is available from the British Library.

ISBN 978 0 7509 6220 9

Typesetting and origination by The History Press
Printed in Great Britain

CONTENTS

INTRODUCTION

Britain may have lost much of her Empire by the 1960s, but she discovered the mini-skirt, boutiques, discos, the Beatles, and unprecedented conflict between the generations. It was the best time for being young, and yes, I was there, and yes, I do remember it! I remember the Summer of Love and the assassination of President Kennedy. I remember Hare Krishna and Vietnam. I remember Minis and feminist protests. I remember the men on the moon, England's World Cup victory and the Moors Murders. I remember the first Notting Hill Carnival and the skirmishes between Mods and Rockers. This was an age of contrasts, when teenagers, the working class and Northerners gained a voice, and the poor arrived in literature and on film. The *New York Times* put it rather differently – in May 1966, London was described as 'the new Sodom and Gomorrah'.

What follows is an insight into the real 1960s, its movers and shakers, its ups and downs, the emphasis on a country that had thrown off the drabness of the post-war 1950s and was determined to enjoy itself. Hopefully, you will find a few surprises along the way.

For instance, the growth in universities – twenty-two were established during the 1960s – was offset by the anti-University in Rivington Street, Shoreditch (London), which charged the teachers and paid the students! It opened in February 1968, and Yoko Ono was a visiting lecturer here, but the concept only lasted for two years in spite of courses that included revolution, black power, joint-rolling and 'how to stay alive'.

To get you in the mood, here are some of the words that were introduced during this fascinating decade:

Cool
Far Out
Karma
Uptight
Vibe
Rip-off
Crash out
Dig
Groovy
Gas (as in fun)

A bibliography would fill far too many pages, as would a list of websites, as all the information that follows has more than one source – an essential requirement for researchers. Special mention, however, goes to Nick Skinner (www.southendtimeline.com) and Peter Brown (www.thesoutheastecho.co.uk). Illustrations are mainly provided by Clipart with thanks also due to Ashley Ferguson for some particularly apposite additional material. Thanks, too, are due to Michelle Tilling at The History Press for having faith in the decade and its power to inspire and entertain. This project has been a labour of love.

1

MUSIC & MUSICIANS

STARTING WITH THE BEATLES – OF COURSE

Having been The Quarrymen in the 1950s, the early (1960) band evolved into The Beetals (sources offer various spellings) who failed an audition to back Billy Fury on tour, and who were then known as The Silver Beetals (or Beetles or Beatles). One story suggests that Billy Fury in fact offered them the job but only on condition they fired then-guitarist Stuart Sutcliffe, but they refused. Recorded in Hamburg, their first release as The Beatles (or, as per the label on the record, The Beat Brothers, adapted for the German audience) was 'My Bonnie' in 1961, with Tony Sheridan then lead vocal. They were not the first Liverpool act to play the Hamburg clubs (1960) – the first were rather less well-known: Derry and the Seniors.

It seems they had their first trademark haircuts in Paris in 1961, copied from French actor Jean Marais in French film *The Testament of Orpheus.*

SOME BEATLES 'FIRSTS'

· debuted at the Cavern Club (Liverpool) in April 1961.

· Brian Epstein, their eventual manager, saw his first Beatles concert at the Cavern in November 1961.

· their first recording session at Abbey Road (for EMI) was in September 1962, with 'Love Me Do'.

· their first national television appearance was 11 January 1963 on *Thank Your Lucky Stars*, performing 'Please Please Me' although they had appeared a few times in 1962 on Granada's *People and Places*.

· first UK No. 1 (in all the charts) was 'From Me To You' in 1963.

· February 1963 was their first British tour, headlined by Helen Shapiro, and starting out at the Gaumont in Bradford.

· Lennon and McCartney wrote Cilla Black's first hit (1963) 'Love of the Loved'.

· 'She Loves You' (1963) was their first single to sell over a million copies – Ozzy Osbourne is among those who claim this was their first record purchase.

· the first Beatles track played in the US was by DJ 'Murray the K' in September 1963 – also 'She Loves You'.

· their first appearance at the Royal Variety Performance in 1963 (at the Prince of Wales Theatre in London) was said to attract over 40 per cent of the British public as viewers – it is when John Lennon famously told the part of the audience in the expensive seats to 'rattle yer jewellery' as a form of applause.

· some 25,000 fans were waiting to see The Beatles at John F. Kennedy Airport when they arrived for their first US visit on 7 February 1964. It seems that the pilot on this flight wore a Beatles wig to mark the occasion.

· a record 73 million viewers tuned in to the *Ed Sullivan Show* on 9 February 1964 for The Beatles' first appearance on US television – with a reputed result of a drop in the US crime rate.

· 'I Want to Hold your Hand' (1964) was their first US hit, selling 12 million copies (in New York alone they were selling 10,000 copies per hour at one stage).

· in March 1964, they became the first 'rock stars' to appear in Madame Tussaud's in London – and went on to use the wax images on the cover of the *Sergeant Pepper* album.

· they debuted on *Top of the Pops* on 25 March 1964.

· they met Elvis for the first time on 27 August 1965 in Beverly Hills and were reputedly so in awe that they were tongue-tied (yep, even John).

· when the Beatles received their MBEs at Buckingham Palace in October 1965 they were the first music band to achieve the accolade, which could have been prompted by Harold Wilson's desire for popularity in the polls. However, it prompted others – such as military personnel – to return their hard-earned MBEs in disgust. In turn, John returned his in 1969 in protest against what was happening in Vietnam and against British involvement in the Nigerian Civil War.

. . . AND SOME BEATLES LASTS

· the Beatles' last appearance at the Cavern Club was in August 1963.

· their last official concert in the US was in Candlestick Park, San Francisco, in August 1966, which could have gone better as they had by now incurred the wrath of the Bible Belt (owing to John's comment about being more popular than Jesus) and even the Klu Klux Klan.

· their last live 'performance' was on the roof of the Apple building in London, singing 'Get Back' on 30 January 1969 –nearby office workers complained to the police about the noise!

· the last album they recorded was 'Abbey Road' in 1969, although 'Let it Be' was the last released.

FOXY FACTS ABOUT EACH OF THE FAB FOUR

John Lennon – told the *Evening Standard* in 1966 that, prophetically, he was 'afraid of growing old'. He appeared on the launch cover of *Rolling Stone* magazine in November 1967. With Yoko Ono at his side, he began their bed-in for world peace in March 1969 at the Hilton Hotel in Amsterdam.

Paul McCartney – met Jane Asher (who became his fiancée) in April 1963 at the Royal Albert Hall, where The Beatles were appearing in *Swingin' Sound* for the BBC. He apparently wrote 'Lovely Rita' (introducing the term Meter Maid to the Brits) after getting a parking ticket from a female warden on Abbey Road in 1967. Although Paul was the last of the Beatles to try LSD, he was the first 'out of the closet' in 1967, declaring the drug a 'universal cure-all'.

George Harrison – was deported from Germany in 1960 because he was too young to be working there (followed home by the other three). He was the first Beatle to visit the USA when he went to see his aunt in Illinois in 1963. His use of a sitar on 'Norwegian Wood' in 1965 was several years before The Beatles visited India. Two years later, on New Year's Day 1967, he was banned from Annabel's in Berkeley Square, London, for not wearing a tie, even though the doorman recognised him.

Ringo Starr – is a lifelong vegetarian. He was the one to come up with the name *A Hard Day's Night* for The Beatles' first film in 1964 (rather than the working title, the more predictable 'Beatlemania'). His song 'Octopus's Garden' (on the *Abbey Road* album in 1969) was composed while on holiday on Peter Sellers' yacht.

. . . AND SOME NON-FAN STORIES

When the Beatles played at the Birkenhead YMCA in 1962 for just £30 (the same year Decca famously turned them down because groups with guitars were on their way out), they were booed off stage. Now you know what Birkenhead and Decca have in common.

In 1966, the Beatles were forced to flee Manila in the Philippines after they were said to have refused to have tea with the President's wife, Imelda Marcos. They denied all knowledge of the invitation – but in any case, would she have wanted them to drink it out of one of her 3,000 pairs of shoes?

MOVING ON TO THE ROLLING STONES

The Stones had a different following to the cuddly, scrubbed-up Beatles – scruffier perhaps? Or raunchier? More rebellious? Their very first single in 1963, 'Come On', reached the charts, and their second was also a hit: 'I Wanna be Your Man' written by . . . Lennon and McCartney. Their first UK No. 1 was 'It's All Over Now' in July 1964.

The Stones' manager, Andrew Oldham, was more rock 'n' roll than the suited-and-booted Brian Epstein, and had an early run-in with the BBC when one radio producer suggested he 'get rid of the singer with the tyre tread lips'.

The first Stones cartoon in a national newspaper appeared in the *Daily Mirror* in December 1963, by Stanley 'Franklin' – effectively announcing their arrival as a pop force to be reckoned with. This was especially the case when Jagger and Richards started writing their own material, the first time being, a tad confusingly, 'The Last Time' (1965).

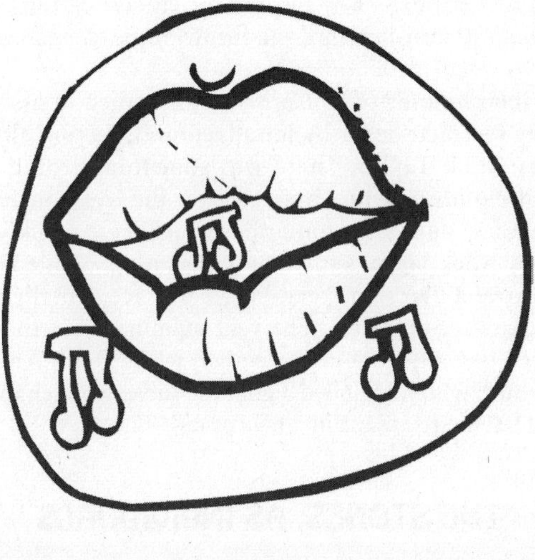

The group were paid £157 10*s* for forming the panel on *Juke Box Jury* in June 1964. A few months later, they turned up on the *Ed Sullivan Show* in the USA but there were so many complaints that Ed Sullivan vowed he would never have them back – although he did, several times. In January 1967, for instance, when they had to change the lyrics of 'Let's Spend the Night Together' replacing 'the night' with 'some time'.

In November 1964, they were banned from BBC Radio after turning up late for *Top Gear* and *Saturday Club*.

The 1967 album cover for *Their Satanic Majesties Request* featured pictures of The Beatles hidden in the undergrowth (returning the compliment of the 'Welcome The Rolling Stones' shirt on a doll featured on the cover of the *Sergeant Pepper* album).

After appearing on *The London Palladium Show* in January 1967, they were the first – and probably the only – stars to refuse to stand on the revolving stage for the programme's finale. Bet they don't like roller coasters, either.

In 1968, they did not get their wish for a graffiti-covered loo to appear on the cover of their *Beggars' Banquet* album, but vented their frustration to some extent by turning the launch (at the Queensgate Hotel in London) into a custard-pie-throwing extravaganza.

1969 was their *annus horribilis*. Brian Jones died in his swimming pool in July (verdict: death by misadventure), having already been replaced by Mick Taylor. There was something ironic about the releasing of clouds of white butterflies at the free concert given in Hyde Park a few days later, butterflies which were quickly trampled underfoot by Mick Jagger's trademark posturing. While filming *Ned Kelly* in Australia that same year, Jagger was accidentally shot in the hand by a back-firing pistol. The year culminated in their final US performance in California in December, when Hell's Angels bikers stabbed a youth who had pulled a gun, the subsequent chaos resulting in the band having to escape in a helicopter.

THE STONES, AS INDIVIDUALS

Brian Jones bought Crotchford Farm, or 'The House at Pooh Corner' – where the Winnie the Pooh stories were written – in 1968. Its 10 acres and woodland cost him £38,000.

Charlie Watts' uncle is Lennie Peters, the blind half of Peters and Lee who came to success in the 1970s – in the '60s, Peters was a pub pianist, and legend has it that he once dismissed Charlie from one of his pub bands for playing too much jazz.

Mick Jagger's first celebrity girlfriend (pre-Marianne Faithfull) was Chrissie Shrimpton, sister of model Jean Shrimpton.

Bill Wyman was the first Rolling Stone to get divorced – in 1969, after ten years of marriage. (He was also, of course, the first to marry.)

Ian Stewart on keyboard was a member of the group from 1962 to 1963, being then effectively demoted to road manager and session pianist 'because his face didn't fit'.

IT WASN'T ALL POP AND ROCK . . .

There was **folk** singing, personified by American Joan Baez, the best-known female of the genre during the decade. She only had one top ten hit in the UK in the 1960s, however – 'There But For Fortune' in 1965. Home-grown (well, Welsh) winner of *Opportunity Knocks*, Mary Hopkin, managed a No. 1 in 1968 with 'Those Were the Days', with the help of Paul McCartney who produced it for the new Apple record label. Switching gender, Bob Dylan (icon of the anti-Vietnam movement) had his first British hit with 'Times they are a-Changing' in 1965 – but he never had a No. 1 single. He did have the first British No. 1 album by a folk singer a year or so earlier, though: *The Freewheelin' Bob Dylan* but in 1966 he was booed off the stage of the Royal Albert Hall in London with cries of 'Judas' after using an electric guitar instead of the traditional acoustic. His British equivalent was, arguably, Donovan, who debuted at No. 4 the same year with 'Catch The Wind' – Donovan was the first of a series of British pop stars to be arrested in 1966 for possession of marijuana, and he was as a result refused entry to the USA in time for the first annual Monterey Festival in 1967. The Seekers were an Australian folk group who had two British number ones in 1965 but had a short-lived career together (1964–8). Frederik Jan Gustav Floris, Baron Van Pallandt (!), son of a Dutch ambassador to Denmark, was one half of the Nina and Frederik duo who were also short-lived but successful enough ('Little Donkey', etc.) to merit their own British television series in 1961.

Jazz in the UK meant two names in hit record terms – traditionalists Kenny Ball and Acker Bilk. Kenny Ball had his biggest hit with 'Midnight in Moscow' in 1961 (reached No. 2) and became the first British jazzman to be honoured with citizenship of New Orleans. Acker Bilk had learned clarinet while serving a three-month sentence in an army prison (for falling asleep while on guard). His 1961 hit 'Stranger on the Shore' also reached No. 2 but spent an impressive 55 consecutive weeks in the charts – this was not its original title but was changed (from Jenny, his daughter's name) when the tune was used for a children's television series of this name. This melody has become the all-time best-selling instrumental in the UK and was the first UK record to reach No. 1 in the USA. In 1969, this was one of the tapes taken to the moon by the Apollo 10 crew!

Other **instrumental** successes included 'Telstar' by the Tornados, Billy Fury's on-off backing group (No. 1 in 1962 and the first single by a UK group to top the US chart), 'Apache' by The Shadows in 1960 (the first of their fourteen Top Ten hits in the '60s, the first backing group to reach No. 1), and 'Albatross' by Fleetwood Mac (reached No. 1 in 1968). American soul band Booker T & the MGs had a huge club success with 'Green Onions', especially among the mod fraternity, but it was not a chart hit until the 1970s. Another American who made an impact was Herb Alpert with his Tijuana Brass – their 'Spanish Flea' made the top three in 1966 and they were the band behind the soundtrack on *Casino Royale* in 1967.

Classical music was not overlooked. Pavarotti made his operatic debut in *La Bohème* in April 1961 at the Teatro Municipale, Reggio Emilia, Italy, with his first performance in the same opera at Covent Garden two years later. In 1962, Benjamin Britten performed his 'War Requiem' in the reconsecrated Coventry Cathedral, with First World War poetry set to music. Maria Callas chose Covent Garden for her last operatic performance in July 1965 in *Tosca*. 1966 brought what was described as one of the great operatic disasters of all time: *Antony and Cleopatra* at the new, huge, and astronomically expensive Metropolitan Opera House in New York, complete with erratic lighting and malfunctioning props and scenery. 1967 brought the controversial Harrison Birtwhistle's violent chamber opera of *Punch and Judy* to the Aldeburgh Festival.

THE BIRTH AND DEATH OF PIRATE RADIO

Until the arrival of offshore private radio, Radio Luxembourg was the only English-speaking commercial radio station that could be heard in the UK – unless you lived in the Isle of Man which had its own laws and its own commercial radio station from early 1964.

The most famous of the pirate stations was Radio Caroline – because it was the first (March 1964) and also because it famously ran aground in 1966 necessitating the rescue of five disc jockeys. Simon Dee was the first pirate DJ, real name Cyril Nicholas Henty-Dodd!

Other pre-1970 pirate radio stations:

Radio Atlanta (merged with Caroline)
Radio Pamela (short-range and short-lived)
Radio London
Radio Sutch*
Radio Essex
Radio Scotland
Radio England
Radio King
Radio City (used same site as Radio Sutch)
Radio 270
Radio 390
Britain Radio

* this was based on the Shivering Sands fort off Whitstable, and hosted by David Sutch who changed his name by deed poll to Screaming Lord Sutch (3rd Earl of Harrow) and later led the Monster Raving Loony Party.

The 1967 Marine Broadcasting Act made it illegal for British companies to advertise on pirate radio stations, starving them out of the water. The BBC quickly realised the potential and kicked off their new popular music channel, Radio 1, just days later. Ex-pirate Tony Blackburn (of Radio Caroline and Radio London) kicked off the station at the helm of their Breakfast Show. His first offering was 'Flowers in the Rain' by The Move. Blackburn was one of seventeen former pirates recruited by the BBC and went on to have a couple of minor hits of his own at the tail-end of the '60s.

MUSICAL BIRTHS . . .

1960 Bono
Mick Hucknall
Kim Wilde
1961 Susan Boyle (yes, that one)
Alison Moyet
Martin Kemp (Spandau Ballet)
Boy George
1962 Jon Bon Jovi
1963 George Michael
Julian Lennon
1964 Lenny Kravitz
1965 Heather Small (ex-M People)
1966 Rick Astley
Marti Pellow
1967 Noel Gallagher
1968 Jason Donovan
Kylie Minogue
Luke and Matt Goss (Bros)
1969 Jay Kay (Jamiroquai)

. . . AND DEATHS

1960 Eddie Cochran (died in Chippenham, following a car crash in which Gene Vincent was also badly injured; 'Three Steps to Heaven' became a posthumous No. 1)
1961 George 'When I'm Cleaning Windows' Formby
Sir Thomas Beecham, composer
1962 Stuart Sutcliffe, original Beatles bassist
1963 Patsy Cline's plane crashed when she was on her way back to Nashville after going to a funeral
1964 Jim Reeves, also killed in a plane crash
Cyril Davies, one of the first UK blues harmonica players
1965 Nat King Cole
1966 Johnny Kidd (of the Pirates) killed in a car crash
Alma Cogan, arguably the first British female pop star
Mike Millward of The Fourmost
1967 Otis Redding, another victim of a plane crash
1968 Bud 'Underneath the Arches' Flanagan
1969 Brian Jones
Billy Cotton of *The Billy Cotton Band Show*

BANNED!

These may seem tame by today's standards, but, in spite of its claim to be the 'permissive society', the decade saw the following records banned by the BBC:

'Tell Laura I Love Her' by Ricky Valance in 1960 was about death, i.e. a no-no as a form of entertainment. The fuss resulted in a No. 1 for the unknown Welsh lad.

Adam Faith's 'Made You' was one of the tracks from his 1960 film *Beat Girl*, but was banned for its sexual connotations.

In 1961, the song 'One Hundred Pounds of Clay' (by Gene McDaniels) was banned because it was considered blasphemous to suggest that women were constructed in the way that buildings were. Came as a bit of a shock to the ex-choir boy from the US but didn't do his career any harm.

Joe Brown's 1963 cover of George Formby's 'With My Little Ukulele in My Hand' was regarded as risqué! Joe had also played guitar on 'Made You' so he was acquiring a bit of a reputation.

Twinkle had a top five hit in 1964 with 'Tommy', helped by its ban due to controversial lyrics about a biker killed in a road accident. This was a British 'version' of the Shangri-Las' US hit 'Leader of the Pack', which was also banned.

'A Day in The Life' was a track from *Sergeant Pepper's Lonely Hearts Club Band* (by the Beatles of course) in 1967, but the BBC was unhappy about its supposed drug references, e.g. 'turn you on'.

Another 1967 Beatles B-side, 'I Am The Walrus', did not go down too well with its use of the word 'knickers'. Shocking.

Reg Presley and The Troggs were in trouble with the BBC in 1967 for their 'lewdly suggestive sounds' on 'I Can't Control Myself' although there does not seem to have been an official ban, just restricted play. It still reached No. 2 though.

'Je t'Aime . . . Moi Non Plus' by Jane Birkin and Serge Gainsbourg joined the list in 1969, because of its sexual connotations.

'Wet Dream' by reggae artist Max Romeo in 1969 was too explicit for Auntie, but the ban sent it to No. 10 and it was a big hit in Jamaica.

A DIFFERENT LOOK AT OTHER GROUPS

Herman's Hermits had only one No. 1 in the 1960s with 'I'm Into Something Good' but two in the USA – 'Mrs Brown, You've Got a Lovely Daughter' and 'I'm Henry the Eighth I am'.

The Bachelors' easy-listening approach to music resulted in eight top ten hits in the '60s, with 1964 their most successful year when they were in the charts for more weeks than The Beatles.

'Juliet' by **The Four Pennies** was the only 1964 chart-topper not to achieve success in America.

The Animals' 'House of the Rising Sun' in 1964 was the first record to hit No. 1 at over four minutes long.

Surprisingly, **The Who**, while epitomising the '60s with 'My Generation', never had a No. 1 on either side of the Atlantic.

Manfred Mann wrote '5-4-3-2-1' as the theme song for the ground-breaking TV show *Ready Steady Go!* in 1964.

Shane Fenton and the Fentones (whose highest chart entry was No. 19 in June 1962 with 'Cindy's Birthday') lost their lead singer with rheumatic disease (Johnny Theakstone, aged just seventeen) and the roadie stepped into the breach before their first success, taking on the Shane Fenton mantle (and he later became Alvin Stardust).

Dave Dee of **Dave Dee, Dozy, Beaky, Mick and Tich** (peaking in 1968 with the No. 1 'Legend of Xanadu' but with a dozen other chart successes) was a police cadet in 1960 and one of the first on the scene of the car crash in which Eddie Cochran died.

'Long Tall Sally' was the name of the debut 1964 single by **The Kinks** which ended up as the name of a chain of shops selling clothes for tall women.

Gerry and the Pacemakers were the first Liverpool group to top the charts in April 1963 (over a month before The Beatles) – with 'How Do You Do It?' They were also the first group to have three consecutive No. 1s with their first three releases.

When **Led Zeppelin** formed in August 1968 from the ashes of The New Yardbirds, the new name came from Keith Moon (the Who's drummer) who thought they would go down 'like a lead balloon'!

The first reggae record to top the UK charts was **Desmond Dekker and the Aces** in 1969, with 'The Israelites'.

When **The Dave Clark Five** had a hit with 'Glad All Over' in 1963, it was banned from football grounds owing to the risk of potential damage of thousands of feet stamping along with the chorus.

Procol Harum is the misspelling of the name of a friend's Burmese cat called Procul Harun (the Latin for 'beyond these things'), but this error did not stop them from having a monster hit with 'A Whiter Shade of Pale' in 1967, partly inspired by Bach's 'Air on a G-String'.

The Hollies had an amazing 21 consecutive top twenty British hit singles from August 1963 onwards – but just one No. 1 in 1965 with 'I'm Alive'.

Although **Cream** were around for less than three years – 1966 to 1969 – all six of their albums reached the top ten, with their final album ('Farewell' in 1969) reaching No. 1 – but, rather oddly, they didn't chart above No. 11 with their singles.

MORE THAN JUST GROUPS

John Leyton had a No. 1 in 1961 with 'Johnny Remember Me', a song he had sung in his role as Johnny St Cyr (i.e. 'sincere'!) in *Harpers West One* on ITV, kick-starting a new career for him in the pop world.

Someone else who crossed over from acting to singing was **Petula Clark** who had her first No. 1 in 1961 with 'Sailor' and another in 1967 with 'This is My Song', although she is better known for the song that just missed the top spot in 1962, reaching No. 2, namely 'Downtown'.

Helen Shapiro was the youngest ever female singer to have a British No. 1, achieved before she even owned a record player. This was in 1961 when she was aged just 14: you don't know the song? It was . . . 'You Don't Know' closely followed by 'Walking Back to Happiness' making her the first female artist to have two consecutive No. 1 hits.

The first UK artist to achieve three consecutive No. 1 hits was **Frank Ifield** – 'I Remember You' and 'Lovesick Blues' in 1962, followed by 'Wayward Wind' in 1963.

1964 was the year that **Cilla Black** had her only two No. 1s – 'Anyone Who Had a Heart' and 'You're My World'. It was also the year that the 'Golden Girl of Pop', **Kathy Kirby**, secured a deal making her the highest paid singer of her generation – reputedly over £1,000 per edition of the *Kathy Kirby Show*, which pulled in audiences around the 20 million mark.

Tom Jones reached No. 1 with a song that had been turned down by Sandie Shaw – this was 'It's Not Unusual' in 1965, his first release 'Chills and Fever' in 1964 being long forgotten.

Sandie Shaw was probably not too worried, though, because she became the first female singer to have three British No. 1s with 'Always Something There to Remind Me' in 1964, 'Long Live Love' in 1965 and 'Puppet on a String' in 1967 which won her – the first UK singer to manage it – the Eurovision Song Contest in Vienna.

The venue for the contest was the Royal Albert Hall in London and luminaries such as Kathy Kirby (1965) and Matt Monro (1964) achieved second place.

The Beatles managed 21 Top 10 hits in the UK in the 1960s.

Ken Dood managed to outsell The Beatles – in 1965, anyway – with 'Tears'.

The only UK No. 1 for 'The White Queen of Soul', aka **Dusty Springfield,** was 'You Don't Have to Say You Love Me' in 1966.

'Please Release Me' hit a record 56 consecutive weeks in the charts between 1967 and 1968 for **Engelbert Humperdinck**.

The UK's biggest seller in 1968 was 'What a Wonderful World' by ageing American **Louis Armstrong**, 67, the oldest person to have a British No. 1.

Although **Matt Monro** only made it to No. 3 during his all-too-brief career (with 'Portrait of My Love' in 1960), Parlophone released 19 successful singles, eight EPs and four LPs between 1960 and 1966 alone. Often compared with Frank Sinatra, he was the toast of America, had his own television series in this country in 1961, became the 'king of the jingles' because of his huge amount of voice-over work, and released 'Yesterday' (1965) before The Beatles.

Another surprising entry on any list of 'those who didn't make it to No. 1' is **Billy Fury**, who was Decca's most charted recording star in the 1960s. He came close with 'Jealousy', a No. 2 in 1961.

THEN THERE WERE THE NOVELTY SONGS

These songs, and artistes, were rather more forgettable . . .

All together now . . . 'Itsy Bitsy Teeny Weeny Yellow Polka Dot Bikini' was a 1960 hit for Brian Hyland and did wonders for burgeoning bikini sales.

Unlikely songstress Sophia Loren teamed up with Peter Sellers in 1960 for 'Goodness Gracious Me' followed a year later by 'Bangers and Mash' – both successes, pre-political correctness.

Comedian Charlie Drake released eleven records during the 1960s, achieving the top twenty with 'Mr Custer' and 'My Boomerang Won't Come Back'.

'Come Outside' reached No. 1 in 1962 featuring a then-unknown Wendy Richard, ten years before she starred in *Are You Being Served?*

Bernard Cribbins' comedy hit of 1962, 'Right Said Fred', went on to inspire the name of a 1990s band, although his other hit of the same year, 'Hole in the Ground', did . . . not.

'Dominique' by the Singing Nun from Belgium was a hit in 1963. Sister Luc Gabrielle left the convent to find fame and fortune in 1967 but it didn't happen.

Dora Bryan's 'All I Want for Christmas is a Beatle' managed the top 40 in December 1963.

Actor Peter Sellers recorded The Beatles' 'A Hard Day's Night' in the style of Richard III and it became a top twenty hit in 1965.

1969 was the year that a three-year-old entered the charts – Microbe (real name Ian Doody) with 'Groovy Baby'. Bless.

SOME SIXTIES SURPRISES

Elvis Presley arrived in Britain in March 1960 – but only got as far as Prestwick Airport in Glasgow, a stop-over to refuel on his return from service in the US Army. The airport opened an Elvis Bar in memory of this magic moment. Although he never returned, this did not deter fans from buying his records, and Elvis had eleven No. 1 hits in the following five years alone – from the UK's then-fastest million-seller 'It's Now or Never' (November 1960) to 'Crying in the Chapel' in 1965, after a two-year absence.

Bruce Forsyth tried for a hit with 'I'm Backing Britain' in 1968, but the song only sold around 7,500 copies – the campaign was not helped by the fact that the Union Jack t-shirts emblazoned with 'I'm Backing Britain' had been made in Portugal.

The Who's reputation for smashing equipment started with an accident. Pete Townshend broke the neck of his guitar on the low ceiling of Harrow's Railway Tavern in 1964 by misjudging the height . . . and the rest is, well, mayhem. Their most dangerous performance was one they gave on the *Smothers Brothers* show (in the USA) in September 1967 when Keith Moon used too much flash powder to explode in a drum: the result, a demolished drum kit, and a singed and deafened Pete Townshend.

The winner of a Mick Jagger impersonation contest at Greenwich Town Hall in 1964 was 16-year-old Chris Jagger. Who said cheat?

The best-selling albums in the UK in 1960 and 1962 respectively were the soundtracks of *South Pacific* and *West Side Story*, overtaken by *The Sound of Music* soundtrack that was the best seller in 1965, 1966 (in the top two every week) and 1968.

Rod Stewart failed the audition to replace Paul Jones when Paul left Manfred Mann in 1966 for a solo career. Instead they chose Mike D'Abo.

The Dave Clark Five were more successful in the USA than in the UK, with seventeen successive Top 40 Billboard chart hits between 1964 and 1967, and eighteen appearances on the *Ed Sullivan Show*.

Roy Wood, who wrote the successful 'Flowers in the Rain' for The Move in 1967, has missed out on royalties ever since because Harold Wilson sued Regal Zonophone over its use of a promotional cartoon featuring the Prime Minister in bed with someone other than his wife. The judge found in Wilson's favour and decreed that all future royalties should go to charity.

Adam Faith cancelled his concerts in South Africa in 1965 after being denied permission to perform in front of multi-racial audiences.

The Cavern Club was sold in February 1966 after the bailiffs had moved in, and reopened in July by Harold Wilson, the Prime Minister. Its new owners presented him with a pipe made out of the wood of the old stage.

'The Twist' is of course associated with American Chubby Checker who had such a hit in 1960, but it was first recorded by Hank Ballard and the Midnighters, and was popular enough to become a 1962 EP *Twist With Victor Silvester* – the dance orchestra leader.

When the Tamla-Motown sound arrived for a tour in 1965 – Stevie Wonder, Smokey Robinson and the Miracles, Martha and the Vandellas, The Supremes – they toured local Odeons and Gaumonts to small audiences. Mary Wilson (ex-Supreme), for one, voiced her disappointment not just with the turnout but with the burgers, the lack of ice, the hot beer, the poor weather and the unforgiving toilet paper!

THE SUMMERS OF LOVE

The Monterey Pop Festival in June 1967 in California became the template for many to follow suit, the first rock festival to attract over 200,000 people – and launching the careers of such stars as Jimi Hendrix (who famously doused his guitar with lighter fuel) and Janis Joplin. British rockers The Who and The Animals also featured. Britain had its own much smaller (some 20,000) version that year – at Woburn, making a big profit for the Duke of Bedford, and regarded by one hippie quoted in the *Sunday Mirror* as a 'cash-in, not a love-in . . . the hot dogs were 1*s* 9*d*'. Here the bands were home-grown only, many appealing to the growing Mod fraternity: The Small Faces, Eric Burdon, Alan Price, Zoot Money, and the unexpected (i.e. poppy) Marmalade.

The sound system for New York's Woodstock in 1969 was designed by Bill 'Rock around the Clock' Haley and the Comets but may not have been suitably appreciated by the crush of 500,000 bodies who tore down the fences, meaning that any hopes of attempting to charge admission fees were abandoned. When 'Food For Love' began to run out of burgers and quadrupled the price, the stand was burned down as being against the spirit of the festival. In the UK, the second Isle of Wight Festival also took place in 1969 with 150,000 in attendance compared to just 10,000 in 1968 – partly no doubt due to the presence of Bob Dylan in his first live performance for three years following a motorbike accident. This was much more of a hippie event than a Mod event with the number of boats needed to ferry fans across the Solent described as a 'second Dunkirk'.

2

FASHION & STYLE

DECADE FIRSTS

The first Doc Martens were introduced on April Fool's Day 1960 (hence the 1460 boot) but soon moved away from their initial market – postmen and policemen. Black leather was replaced with red, and they became popular with the new breed of youth, taking over from winkle-pickers. A few years later, competition came from Hush Puppies and from knee-high boots – white, for preference.

Estée Lauder began to expand her American cosmetic business into Europe (and beyond) in 1960, her first contract being with Harrods in Knightsbridge. In 1962, she began the now-popular practice of selecting a face (usually a model) for the brand.

Jackie Kennedy introduced Brits to the pillbox hat and to three-quarter-length sleeves in the early part of the decade.

Tights were introduced into Britain (thanks to the invention of Lycra) in 1960, in time for mini-skirts. They went on sale in Marks and Spencer for the first time in 1962.

Crimplene and Trevira arrived in 1961, girdles were first patented in 1964, and dresses made of paper or plastic had a brief life between 1965 and 1967.

Bikinis became hugely popular (although a decade old) after Ursula Andress's damp appearance in *Dr No* (1962) and Frankie Avalon's movie, *Beach Party* (1963). Similarly, berets had a revival as a result of Faye Dunaway's distinctive look in *Bonnie and Clyde* (1967).

For men, pre-washed jeans appeared in the '60s in Britain as did bell-bottoms, Paisley shirts, military wear and crushed velvet trousers. Even Barbie's boyfriend, Ken, wore a Paisley shirt.

Mini-skirts, although popularised by Mary Quant, had already been introduced by John Bates and André Courrèges. John Bates became famous for his designs for Diana Rigg in *The Avengers*.

In January 1966, Customs and Excise changed the tax on clothing. Until then, there had been no tax on children's clothing, which had been identified by length. Because mini-skirts were therefore avoiding additional taxes payable on adult clothing, the criteria was changed from length to bust size. Spoilsports.

Long peasant skirts arrived as bras disappeared later in the '60s with the hippie generation. Afghan coats and kaftans were also introduced during this 'flower power' (from *c.* 1967) period.

THE LOOK

Vidal Sassoon introduced short, geometric hairstyles in 1963. Goodbye (for a while at least) to backcombing, false hair, perms, and sleeping in curlers. He was credited with the Nancy Kwan cut (longer in the front than the back), the five-point cut, the layered cut called 'the Shape', and the bob. His styles were popularised by the Queen of the Mods – Cathy McGowan and her shiny bob – and singer Sandie Shaw, as well as by Twiggy and such iconic figures as The Beatles' girlfriends and film stars such as Rita Hayworth and Ava Gardner. Note that Rockers still favoured the bouffant and lacquered look (the girls, that is).

Wigs became acceptable – Beatles wigs followed by afro wigs in particular. Artist Andy Warhol became the most famous proponent of the wig (owning hundreds), although American girl groups such as The Supremes also influenced this trend.

The midi- and the maxi-skirt had both arrived by 1969. A mini-skirt and a maxi-coat were the way to incorporate two disparate looks.

The most popular make-up for the younger set was Miner's, with Rimmel not far behind. Pale lips, lined eye sockets, false or painted-in lashes (á la Twiggy, who in turn had copied the eyes from her rag doll) were an essential part of the look. Mary Quant and Biba both introduced their own make-up lines in the mid-1960s.

For mods (or modernists): made-to-measure suits, Italian and mohair for preference, with the length of the vents being indicative of how on-trend you were (or not). Harrington jackets (named after Rodney Harrington in the *Peyton Place* TV series) were acceptable after Steve McQueen appeared wearing one on the cover of *Life Magazine* in 1963. Additionally, there were Ben Sherman or Fred Perry shirts or striped cycling shirts. Footwear ranged from Hush Puppies to desert boots, mock-croc or bowling shoes. Pork pie hats were worn on scooters before the necessity for helmets. The girls favoured ski-pants, granny shoes with round toes and instep straps, nothing revealing or curvy. No wonder the term Peacock Revolution came into use at this time.

A DOZEN PLACES TO SHOP FOR 'THE LOOK' IN SWINGING LONDON

Biba – a diminutive of Biruta, Barbara Hulanicki's sister. Hulanicki's label started out with a gingham dress available by mail order in 1963 – from the *Daily Mirror* – expecting 300 orders, but actually in receipt of 17,000, so many that Barclays would not accept all the 25*s* postal orders they tried to bank! (The bank account was promptly changed to Nat West.) The first shop was in Abingdon Road, Kensington, then a much larger store in Kensington Church Street in 1969, the most glamorous and decadent in London. Not only clothes, but make-up (purple and plum were very popular for eyes) and even such goodies as Art Nouveau wallpaper to liven up dull 1960s dwellings. Customers included household names like Barbra Streisand, Yoko Ono and Julie Christie. The company did a boom and bust in the 1970s.

Granny Takes a Trip in King's Road, London. Opened in January 1966, Granny catered for late Mods and early hippies – male and female – and drew much of its custom from the pop world.

Mr Fish in Clifford Street in London's West End also opened in 1966, with a label illustrating its 'non-square' style – i.e. 'Peculiar to Mr Fish'. This was one of several shops for the new man which could provide Liberty print shirts (as worn by Terence Stamp in *Modesty Blaise*, 1965) and kipper ties.

John Stephen was the man behind over half a dozen of the 'boutiques' which abounded in London's Carnaby Street by the end of the decade. His first was His Clothes and the location was chosen (at the end of the 1950s) because it was cheap – £10 per week for the rent. Other shops such as John Stephen (naturally) and Mod Male quickly followed. John Stephen himself was a Glaswegian grocer's son in his twenties, unlike the man behind Mr Fish who had started out at the aristocratic Turnbull and Asser in Jermyn Street – one of many illustrations of the erosion of the class system in the 1960s. According to the *Scotsman*, John Stephen is probably the only gay Scot commemorated on a plaque in London – sounds about right.

Laura Ashley's first London shop opened in Pelham Street in South Kensington in 1968, in time for the maxi dress which the label favoured. This label started out from a modest Welsh outlet in 1960 producing utility wear (e.g. gardening smocks) which were being snapped up for social wear.

Bus Stop in Kensington Church Street opened in 1969, the queues on opening day resulting in the shop being emptied of stock by closing time – even the cushions in the window had been sold. Lee Bender was the name behind Bus Stop which survived until 1979.

Bazaar in Knightsbridge was the shop opened by Mary Quant in 1961 (she had another in King's Road opened six years earlier). Want hot pants? This was the place to go from 1969.

The Fulham Road Clothes Shop from 1967 was Zandra Rhodes and her partner's creation during the psychedelic era.

I Was Lord Kitchener's Valet in Portobello Road from 1966 specialised in military wear (and peripherals such as flags) as well as crushed velvet trousers. One regular here was Jimi Hendrix – and the shop inspired both a 1966 song by the New Vaudeville Band, and the cover of Beatles album *Sergeant Pepper's Lonely Hearts Club Band*. Other branches soon followed in London's West End.

The Beatles' Apple Store opened in Baker Street in December 1967 but lasted less than a year although offering both military and hippie gear. The Beatles financed the operation but it was run by a trio of Dutch hippie designers. However, it seems that the high prices and perhaps the location kept the punters away. It closed on 31 July 1968 with huge losses – the remaining stock was given away to passers-by.

430 Kings Road – in 1966, this was Hung On You, with a propensity for hippie clothes, whose owner (Michael Rainey) was married to Lord Harlech's daughter. The same space was taken on in 1969 by Mr Freedom, whose

designer, Tommy Roberts, achieved fame by dressing such pop luminaries as Mick Jagger and Elton John (and continued to expand into Kensington, Carnaby Street and later into Covent Garden).

Quorum, Radnor Walk, off King's Road, was the place to buy Ossie Clark and Celia Birtwell designs. Their catwalk shows featured dancing models to a backdrop of thumping music by such artistes as Jimi Hendrix. Clark was one of the first to use such exotic materials as snakeskin and feathers, and he also introduced a menswear line in 1968 which included a pink crêpe shirt with ruffles, edged in silk. No wonder the shop attracted the new and influential pop clientele – among them the Stones, Cathy McGowan and Pattie Boyd. As rock stars morphed into friends, Ossie named designs after their songs – Little Red Rooster was prompted by the Rolling Stones hit in 1964, and Interstellar Overdrive by Pink Floyd's psychedelic 1966 hit. Note that Ossie's pedigree was literally second to none, in that when he graduated from the Royal College of Art in 1965 with a first-class degree, he was the only one to achieve this level.

INTRODUCING YOUNG STYLE

Department stores, previously catering for debutantes, had to change their image. Woollands in Knightsbridge (long gone) opened the '21 Shop' in-house in 1961, with the Temperance Seven engaged to entertain customers on opening day. Jaeger opened Young Jaeger, Selfridge's countered with Miss Selfridge, and Harrods with Way In.

In London, 2,000 'boutiques' had opened by 1967. There doesn't seem to have been one called Jumping on the Bandwagon, though.

CONTROVERSIAL FASHION

When Mary Quant collected her OBE at Buckingham Palace in 1966, she made a point of wearing a mini-skirt. Of course. More controversially, when interviewed for a series featured in the *Guardian* in 1967 (called 'the Permissive Society') she announced that she had dyed her pubic hair green, and referred to that taboo area as 'the crotch'!

At different times in the 1960s, interior designer David Mlinaric was turned away from the Cavalry Club for wearing a bright pink shirt and from Annabel's Nightclub (both in London) for wearing a white suit.

Similarly, Susannah York was not allowed into the Colony Restaurant in New York in October 1966 because she was wearing a trouser suit. She dutifully returned in a dress, although she had packed another three trouser suits in her suitcase. By 1969, even Princess Anne was wearing a trouser suit – in purple.

STYLE MAKES NEWS

Yves St Laurent split from Christian Dior (where he was Chief Designer) in 1961 and set up under his own name. He opened his first couture house in Paris in 1962 – but he is not in fact French, he is Algerian.

Mary Quant was approached to design for the biggest retail chain in the USA, J.C. Penney, in 1962. She was the first British designer promoted in this way in the US.

In 1967, Vidal Sassoon made headlines in Britain and the USA when he cut Mia Farrow's long blonde hair into a cropped pixie style which was revealed in the film *Rosemary's Baby*. His fee was reputed to have been $5,000. This wasn't his first foray into the tabloids – when he cut 4ft off Nancy Kwan's locks, this too made headlines.

Perhaps even more popular with the paparazzi was Jackie Kennedy's wedding to Greek millionaire Aristotle Onassis in 1968 when she wore a white Valentino mini.

In June 1968, according to the *Telegraph*, Mayfair hairdresser 'Teasy-Weasy' Raymond (who had trained Vidal Sassoon) was refused admission to the Royal Enclosure at Ascot. 'Maybe it's simply not the thing to be a hairdresser,' was his only comment – very restrained – but he was much happier a year later when the ban was lifted.

When American film star Cary Grant bowed out of his motion picture career in 1968, he was snapped up by Fabergé (who had introduced the best-selling Brut aftershave in 1964) as the first of their brand ambassadors. He was attracted by the fact that they had their own jets so he wouldn't have to hide from fans – and he didn't even have to appear in their advertising. Just his name was apparently good enough.

The popular C&A fashion store in Princes Street, Edinburgh, was the first in the city to have CCTV installed. 140 cameras arrived in 1969 over seven floors. All the C&A stores at the time were a port of call for modern and classic fashion – i.e. for all age groups.

STYLE CHOICES

The Mod look was for those who wanted a smart look, one favoured by such '60s bands as The Small Faces. Bespoke suits had to have the requisite number of buttons, vents and pockets. Trends for such individual features as big collars or Paisley shirts came 'in' and 'out' rapidly.

Pop art, with its colourful use of the bull's eye motif was popularised by The Who – bands and music were becoming very influential on fashion. T-shirts – previously regarded pretty much as underwear – featured rock bands and such icons as Che Guevara and so became popular with youngsters from all social backgrounds.

For Rockers, who had mainly evolved from the 1950s Teddy Boys (although Teddy Boy styles were also adapted by Mods), there were predictable black leather jackets, quiffs – and, of course, jeans. Not so much a fashion choice, as an opting-out of fashion.

For Beats/Beatniks (lingering from the 1950s), or Folkies, often followers of CND, the style was Fair Isle or polo-neck sweaters, sandals, tweed caps and beards.

For hippies – later in the decade – long skirts, beads, headbands, body art, flowers and long hair. The influence here was non-Western cultures.

Fashion had only really changed dramatically for the young at this stage. But for mums and dads, too, changes gradually made their way into every home. Modern mums were now wearing less gloves and more trousers and were happily ditching the discomfort of suspenders and stockings, while dads were saying goodbye to traditional headgear.

SEVEN ROLE MODELS

In 1966, when only 16, the *Daily Express* named Twiggy 'The Face of 1966' and described her as 'The Cockney kid with a face to launch a thousand shapes', though she is in fact from north-west London – Neasden in fact – outside the Cockney boundaries. She was the first model to lend her name to products including bags, lunch boxes, pens, false eyelashes and paper dolls, with a Twiggy Barbie doll on sale in 1967. In the same year, she was the first model to be sculpted for Madame Tussaud's in London and she even had a hit record – in Japan – with 'Beautiful Dreams'. Not only that, but Twiggy was the youngest person ever to appear on *This is Your Life* in 1969, aged just 20. She 'retired' from her – first – modelling career in 1969 having been earning as much as £80 per hour when the average weekly wage was £15, and went on to make fifteen films as well as release a few records.

Joanna Lumley, born in India where her father was a major in the Gurkha Rifles, was apparently the muse for classic designer Jean Muir after completing her training at Lucy Clayton's famous modelling agency. Although she failed a RADA audition, she made her way into acting – her first love – via television commercials, following a short-lived but successful modelling career in the 1960s.

Jean Shrimpton was another 1960s supermodel from the Lucy Clayton stable. She is said to have hated her nickname – which was, predictably, 'The Shrimp'. In 1965, she caused a minor sensation at the Melbourne Cup when she wore a mini dress, shocking the Antipodeans. She is better known for her relationships with David Bailey and actor Terence Stamp, but neither relationship lasted very long, because both men were perhaps more interested in themselves than in Jean.

When model Pattie Boyd married Beatle George Harrison in January 1966, her wedding outfit was from Mary Quant – who else? She was the muse not of fashion designers, however, but of songwriters, with both George and her second husband (Eric Clapton) writing songs for her. It also seemed that Pattie's interest in Eastern mysticism inspired first George and then the rest of The Beatles.

Paulene Stone's name may not be as familiar as other supermodels but she had a long and lucrative career spanning the 1960s, and lived the life of a WAG – giving birth to actor Laurence Harvey's daughter, Domino, in 1969 for example.

Penelope Tree was another stick-thin successful 1960s teenage model (still a teenager in fact in 1969). Anglo-American, from a comfortable background, she graced the covers of such magazines as *Vogue*, and had a longer-term-than-usual (for him, if not for her) relationship with photographer David Bailey, who described her as an 'Egyptian Jiminy Cricket'. She was known for her lack of smiles (on camera) and doll-like features.

Verushka, the daughter of a Prussian Count, arrived in New York in 1961 and tried to secure bookings in the name of Vera. This didn't work, so she returned a couple of years later as Veruschka, her 6ft 3in frame dressed in head-to-toe-black, and hey presto! Of all the actresses, models and '60s swingers who featured in Antonioni's cult 1966 film *Blow-Up*, she was the only star to appear as herself.

THE OTHER SIDE OF THE CAMERA

David Bailey – East Ender David Bailey wanted first to be an artist, then Fred Astaire, but ended up as what he once described as 'the next best thing': a fashion photographer. He was working for *Vogue* by the time he was just 22 (in 1960). Although soon in demand for fashion work, and renowned for so many of his iconic photographs of the supermodels of the day, he became just as in demand in the new celebrity world. Marianne Faithfull, Sandie Shaw, Catherine Deneuve (an ex-wife), Michael Caine, even the Kray twins – all have been snapped by the legend that is David Bailey. The film *Blow-Up* is said to be 'based' on his charismatic life – but only he knows whether this is true.

Terence Donovan took his first photograph for *Vogue* in 1963, moving easily from the world of industrial photography to that of fashion. He continued to be associated with them until his death. Donovan is another East Ender who was aware of the change that the Terrible Trio (or Black Trinity – which included Duffy and Bailey) were bringing. To use his words (in the *Sunday Times*) 'we are fat, short and heterosexual', unlike earlier photographers whom he regarded as 'tall, thin and camp'. Subjects included Mary Quant, Julie Christie and Kingsley Amis.

Brian Duffy – not strictly an East Ender, but his family moved to East Ham when he was five (in the 1930s). Duffy set up his London studio in 1963 after working in New York and Paris. He used Morocco as a base for his first famous Pirelli calendar (1966). The boy had spread his wings, but his temperament remained very down-to-earth because of his un-PC views and his strong language. He has been described as the most objectionable, and therefore the most interesting, of the Terrible Trio. Similarly, Joanna Lumley once said of him that he plied his models with wine and made them sing! But for him, he 'wanted to make women look good'.

Patrick Lichfield (or Earl Lichfield) lay aside his title to enter the competitive – but glamorous – world of photography. In common with the Terrible Trio, Lichfield blurred early class boundaries as so often happened in the 1960s. His subjects included Joanna Lumley, Bianca Jagger and Marsha Hunt, the black American model/singer. As a part of the Swinging Sixties, he could be seen in flowing frills, velvet and ruffs. Not averse to making good use of his 'contacts' however, he became rather a specialist when it came to photographing the royal family.

During the 1960s, Antony Armstrong-Jones (or Lord Snowdon) photographed not only Princess Margaret but everyone from Albert Finney to Rudolf Nureyev, Peter Sellers to Barbara Hepworth, and the rest. He was the picture editor of the *Sunday Times* magazine in the early 1960s, and – embracing another arm of his talent – designed a new aviary for London Zoo in the same period.

A DIFFERENT KIND OF STYLE

Interiors were also affected by the end of utilitarianism and an era of new spending power. The first Habitat opened in May 1964 in Fulham Road, London, on the site of the Admiral Keppel pub, just yards away from a greasy spoon and derelict buildings. Early customers included John Lennon, the Duke of Kent, David Niven, George Harrison and Mary Quant (who had designed the staff uniform). Terence Conran, the man behind Habitat, described his store as the 'Mary Quant of the furniture world'. He had been inspired by furniture shops in Scandinavia and displayed goods in a new-look minimal pine interior, stacked in now-familiar warehouse style piles. For the first time, it was easy to buy French cookware, a garlic press or a white plastic chair . . . and Conran has been credited as the man who introduced the duvet to Britain. By 1968, he had four shops in London, and a year later had established outlets in Manchester and Brighton.

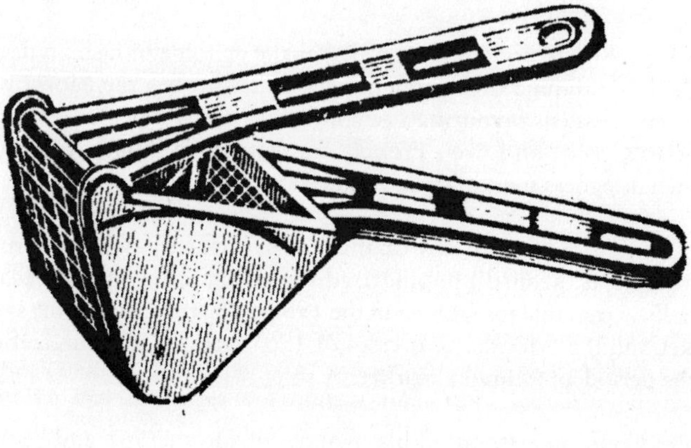

Furniture fads associated with the 1960s included plastic blow-up chairs and the lava lamp with its space-age sputnik shape. The work of artists such as Andy Warhol and Bridget Riley crossed over into interiors including fabrics and wallpapers. Art Nouveau reappeared with a psychedelic edge undreamed of by its earlier originators. Indian and Moroccan influences appealed to the hippie generation at the end of the decade. As more telephones were installed in British homes, the telephone table was also something new on the scene.

Troika pottery opened in 1963 using innovative new finishes and materials – for example, broken glass. Its location, near the beach in St Ives, Cornwall, is now a museum. One of their biggest clients was Heals in Tottenham Court Road, London. Heals itself celebrated its 150th anniversary in 1960, and this was marked by a 'Designers of the Future Exhibition'. Unlike Troika, Heals survives.

In March 1969, Richard Block and David Quayle opened a DIY shop in Southampton (Block and Quayle), when DIY was the hobby of the few. The hobby grew, and the public found the DIY retailer less daunting than entering a builders' merchants . . . so the risk paid off. The name change to B&Q followed soon after.

IKEA opened its first store in Stockholm in 1965, sporting a controversial design inspired by the circular Guggenheim Museum in New York.

THE DEATH OF HAUTE COUTURE?

The French were no longer regarded as the epitome of fashion design in the UK although their influence continued among the Mods, with a *poseur* element favouring French films, French film stars (such as Juliette Greco) and even French cigarettes (Gauloise). However, French designers put up a brave fight:

Yves St Laurent (and Coco Chanel, who, incidentally, regarded the mini-skirt as 'absurd') popularised the trouser suit once it became socially acceptable for women in the 1960s. The trench coat, the safari jacket and the 'Mondrian' dresses of 1965 were all YSL innovations of the period and found a market.

André Courrèges produced his own designs from 1961 and became popular for his silver and white PVC dresses, white catsuits and monochrome wear. Very – and appropriately – space age. His white boots with peep-holes were best-sellers and famously worn to a Buckingham Palace garden party by the leggy blonde twin daughters of Cabinet Minister Douglas Jay.

Paco Rabanne (a Francophile born in Spain) started his own line of design in 1966 using cardboard, paper, acetate and metal. He also introduced woody rather than flowery perfumes, his first appearing in a bottle circled in metal (Calandre) in 1969.

3

CRIME & PUNISHMENT

SEX, DRUGS AND ROCK AND ROLL

Throughout the 1960s, Detective Chief Inspector William Moody, head of the Obscene Publications Squad, not only took money from Soho 'bookshops' to 'prevent' them being raided or closed, but would sell confiscated material at a knock-down price to other 'bookshops'. A nice little earner.

Before 1963, John Profumo's actress wife, Valerie Hobson, was more famous than he was as Secretary of State for War. Once he admitted to lying to the House of Commons about his 'association' with Christine Keeler, things changed! His affair with Christine, at the same time as she was sleeping with Soviet naval attaché Captain Yevgeny Ivanov, and – especially – the fact that he lied to Parliament ended his career. It also sparked the premature resignation of Harold Macmillan, brought down, to his chagrin, by 'two tarts' (the second tart was Mandy Rice-Davies, Keeler's bosom buddy, so to speak) and the suicide of osteopath Stephen Ward, who had been charged with living on immoral earnings at his Wimpole Mews flat, the flat he shared with, variously, Keeler and Rice-Davies. The latter's riposte in court, incidentally, following a client's denial of any untoward relationship (Lord Astor, if you want a name) is often quoted: 'Well, he would, wouldn't he?' Note that Christine Keeler served six months for perjury in another trial – that of another lover, John Edgecombe – but Mandy Rice-Davies escaped, her reputation not exactly intact.

Lady Isabella Frankau (who died in 1967) ran an up-market psychiatric practice in Wimpole Street, London, where, in 1962 alone, she prescribed 600,000 tablets of heroin. [Note: 1,053 heroin addicts were known to the Home Office in 1967, compared to 47 in

1955!] Dr John Petro offered a similar service outside the all-night Boots chemist at Piccadilly Circus, selling prescriptions at £3 apiece until he was arrested and struck off in 1968.

In 1964, Denisa, Lady Newborough, was convicted of allowing her Mayfair maisonette to be used for habitual prostitution, but her conviction was quashed on appeal. For her, this was just another minor embarrassment in a life peopled by such high profile admirers as Adolf Hitler and the King of Spain.

A fan dancer at the Windmill Theatre in London, Janie Jones, was charged with running a brothel in 1967, which also allegedly provided her with people she could blackmail. But she was acquitted and continued with her recording 'career'.

The Rolling Stones could be described as the Rockers in the Dock . . . A précis should include Brian Jones being twice charged with possession of marijuana in 1967 and 1968, resulting in fines and probation (spending just one night in prison at Wormwood Scrubs), and Mick Jagger and Marianne Faithfull being busted for possession of cannabis in 1969 resulting in a fine for Jagger. Additionally, Keith Richards and Jagger were given prison sentences in 1967 following drugs charges in Chichester – where a poster outside the court proclaimed 'Let he who is without sin, jail the first Stone'. Their sentences were quashed after one night in prison – Brixton for Jagger and Wormwood Scrubs for Richards. Jagger's first appearance in court, however, seems to have been for driving without insurance (in Liverpool) in August 1964, resulting in another paltry (for a rock star, that is) fine.

When the police raided Ringo Starr's London flat occupied by John Lennon and Yoko Ono in October 1968 they found only a small amount of marijuana, resulting in a £150 fine. Very affordable.

In September 1969, a hippie commune in 100 rooms at 144 Piccadilly in London was invaded by 200 police investigating the illegal possession of drugs. Over 150 squatters were taken to the police station, although only thirty were charged.

An effort was made in 1969 to crack down on young lovers smooching in public in Inca, Majorca. The police chief handed out citations worth 500 pesetas per kiss. As a result, thirty couples protested with a kiss-in at Cala Figuera harbour, but they were rounded up and fined a total of 45,000 pesetas for their 'defiance'!

Pete Townshend spent a night in prison in New York in 1969 after kicking a plain-clothes policeman who jumped onto the stage to warn The Who that the building was on fire – he claimed he thought he was being attacked.

LOOKING ON THE GRIM SIDE – EXECUTIONS IN THE SIXTIES

John Louis Constantine, 23, at Lincoln on 1 September 1960 for the murder of Lily Parry, 73.

Norman Harris, 23, and Francis 'Flossy' Forsyth (the last 18-year-old hanged in Britain) at two London prisons on 10 October 1960 for murder of Allan Jee, 23.

Anthony Joseph Miller, 19, at Glasgow on 22 December 1960 for the murder of John Cremin, 49. The last teenager executed in the UK and the last hanging at Barlinnie.

Wasyl Gnypiuk, 34, at Lincoln on 27 January 1961 for the murder of his landlady, Louise Surgey, 62 – apparently while dreaming . . .

George Riley, 21, at Shrewsbury on 9 February 1961, for the murder of Adeline Smith, 62 – though he protested his innocence to the end.

Jack Day, 31, at Bedford on 29 March 1961 for the murder of Keith Arthur, 25. Day tried to sue the *Spectator* for libel because they had printed the news of his execution two days earlier . . . but time was not on his side.

Victor Terry, 20, at Wandsworth on 25 May 1961 for the murder of John Pull, 61 (during a raid on Lloyds Bank). This hopeless villain had left his shotgun behind in the back of a taxi used at one stage in his attempt to escape with his accomplices.

Zsiga Pankotia, 31, at Leeds on 29 June 1961 for the murder of Eli Myers, 50, during a bungled burglary. Last person to be executed at Leeds.

Edwin Bush, 21, at Pentonville, on 6 July 1961 for the murder of Elsie Batten, 59. The first time that the Identikit process was used to track down a murderer.

Samuel McLaughlin, 40, at Belfast on 25 July 1961 for the murder of his wife, Maggie, 32, after openly boasting that he killed her to avoid paying maintenance.

Hendryk Niemasz, 49, at Wandsworth on 8 September 1961, for the murder of Hubert and Alice Buxton (35 and 37). He was the last man to be hanged in London – after being sentenced to death and life imprisonment to 'run concurrently'!

Robert McGladdery, 25, at Belfast, on 20 December 1961, for the murder of Pearl Gamble, 19. This was the last execution in Northern Ireland, and the story behind the BBC's 2008 documentary, *Last Man Hanging*.

James Hanratty, 25, at Bedford on 4 April 1962, for the murder of Michael Gregsten, 34: the infamous A6 murder. 2003 DNA tests were said to confirm that he was the A6 killer although many supported him at the time, including John Lennon.

Oswald Grey, 20, at Birmingham, on 20 November 1962, for the murder of Thomas Bates, 47. Grey was the youngest man executed at Birmingham for over a decade.

James Smith, 26, at Manchester, on 28 November 1962, for the murder of Sarah Cross, 57, with evidence picked up for the first time in – a vacuum cleaner.

Henry Burnett, 21, at Aberdeen on 15 August 1963 for the murder of Thomas Guyan, 27. He was the last man to be hanged in Scotland – on Aberdeen's brand new gallows.

Russell Pascoe and Dennis Whitty (24 and 22) at Bristol and Winchester respectively, on 17 December 1963, for the murder of William Rowe, 64. Rowe had been thought dead for the forty years following the First World War after deserting and going into hiding, revealing himself after Queen Elizabeth granted deserters an amnesty!

Peter Allen and Gwynne Evans (21 and 24) at Liverpool and Manchester respectively on 13 August 1964 for the murder of John West, 53. Another bungled burglary, with Evans' raincoat left at the scene, containing a medallion with his name on it. These were the last two men hanged in the UK.

Capital punishment was suspended in 1965 for five years, with a decision not to reintroduce it made at the end of 1969. David Chapman was the last man sentenced to death (at Leeds) on 1 November 1965 and endured a long wait to see whether his punishment would take effect.

FUZZ FACTS

Following the post-war increase in car ownership, the Stolen Motor Vehicle Investigation branch was established in 1960. Vroom, vroom, you're nicked!

The Metropolitan Police established their first police frogman unit in April 1962.

Helicopters were first used by Oxford City Police in 1963 for 'special events' and introduced in the fight against crime in 1967, becoming permanent fixtures five years later.

Following the introduction of London mini-cabs in 1961, the Metropolitan Police obtained two dozen convictions for illegal plying for hire in the first year alone.

In June 1964, Detective Sergeant Harold Challenor was tried at the Old Bailey for conspiracy to pervert the course of justice but found unfit to plead (i.e. as mad as a March hare). As a result, anyone subsequently pretending to be mad in court was known as 'doing a Challenor'.

In 1968, Southern Television showed a young girl being abducted, screaming for help as she was dragged into a car, and ignored by passers-by. The abductors were local police, demonstrating public apathy – very successfully.

Britain's first black policeman joined the Coventry force in June 1966: Kenyan-born Mohamet Yusuf Daar, PC492. The first to join the Met was Norwell Roberts in 1967 who, in spite of having bananas thrown at him from patrol cars, went on to receive the Queen's Police Medal.

Their female counterpart arrived the following year: Jamaican-born Mrs Sislin Allen, who enrolled at the Met's police training centre in Westminster.

The first computer used by the Metropolitan Police was in 1963 – for use on pay and crime statistics.

When personal radios became commonplace at the end of 1969, the familiar blue police boxes (or Dr Who boxes) were redundant, and their destruction was ordered. Exterminate! Exterminate!

LAYING DOWN THE LAW

The following Acts came into force in the 1960s:

The Road Traffic Act of 1960 led to the first traffic wardens – in Westminster. The first ticket was issued to a doctor who claimed he was treating a patient for a heart attack!

The Betting and Gaming Act of 1960 led to the first legal betting shops from May of the following year. Their advertising was so restricted, however, that they were not easy to find – even though as many as 10,000 opened up before the end of 1961. Britain's first legal casino opened in Brighton in June 1962, and, in all, 1,000 casinos opened in the first five years – partly because a loophole in the law meant that almost anyone could open one. The loophole was closed in 1970.

In January, 1960, the Isle of Man's Government raised the legal minimum whipping age from 14 to 21, rendering only adults liable for corporal punishment.

Abortion was legalised by a 1967 Act that came into force in 1968.

A new Criminal Justice Bill in 1967 ruled that majority verdicts would be accepted in court where unanimous decisions were not achieved. The first majority verdict (of 10 to 2) was returned in a Brighton case in October that year when a professional wrestler (the Terrible Turk) was found guilty of stealing a handbag.

And . . . it was the start of a new era with the appointment of Elizabeth Lane, 60, as the first female High Court judge in August 1965. (She had already set precedents as the first female County Court judge and the first female Divorce Commissioner.)

LINGERING INFAMY

The Krays

When Barbara Windsor and the cast of *Sparrers Can't Sing* were filming around Cambridge Heath Road and other parts of the East End in the early 1960s, the Krays were hired to provide security on the set and can be seen – briefly – on screen.

When Reggie Kray married Frances Shea in April 1965 at St James the Great in Bethnal Green Road, the wedding photographer was Leytonstone-born David Bailey, who did the job 'for free'. One of their wedding telegrams was from Judy Garland.

When Ronnie Kray shot and killed George Cornell in the Blind Beggar, Whitechapel Road, in 1966, the record playing on the juke box was 'The Sun Ain't Gonna Shine Anymore' by the Walker Brothers.

The Kray twins' trial at the Old Bailey in 1969 (for the murders of George Cornell and Jack 'The Hat' McVitie) was the Old Bailey's longest criminal trial, lasting thirty-nine days. They also received the longest sentences ever imposed at the Old Bailey – life, with a recommendation that they each serve at least 30 years.

The final piece of music played at Reggie Kray's funeral at St Matthew's Church in Bethnal Green in 2000 was 'My Way'.

The Great Train Robbery

Ronnie Biggs was brought into the 'gang' because he knew a man who could drive the Royal Mail train. The hold-up in Buckinghamshire, which took place on 8 August 1963, involved a haul of some £2.5 million in used banknotes, far more than the million anticipated.

The besieged Post Office train – known as the Up Special – had up until then run every night, without interference, for 125 years.

Leaving their fingerprints behind in the farm used for their preparations was not a clever move – although the robbery itself was well planned. Charmian Biggs' spending spree after the haul was also not a good move – raising suspicions in at least one shop where she flashed the cash.

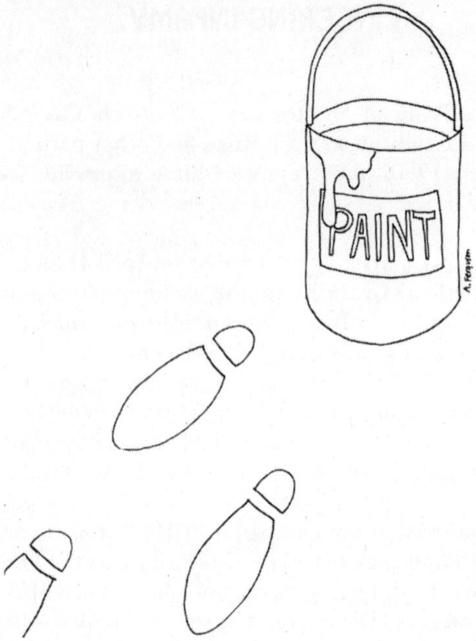

One of those convicted, William Boal, who died in prison, was allegedly innocent. The story goes that the yellow paint on his shoes from a can found at the gang's hideout, Leatherslade Farm, was planted by Detective Chief Superintendent Thomas Butler – known as One-Day Tommy for the speed in which he caught criminals . . .

Charles Wilson escaped from Winson Green on 12 August 1964 (recaptured in Canada in January 1968) and Ronnie Biggs from Wandsworth in July 1965 (and famously gave himself up after 35 years on the run).

Bruce Reynolds (the possible mastermind) managed five years on the run before being caught, in Torquay, in November 1968. Buster Edwards gave himself up after three years on the run.

Although twelve members of the gang were convicted in 1964, James White was not arrested until 1966 when thousands of £25 notes were found hidden in his caravan.

The Moors Murders
Ian Brady showed an early interest in Nazi war crimes and the works of the Marquis de Sade. A few clues here.

Photos taken of Myra Hindley by Brady on the moors, following their gruesome murders, often featured her dog, Puppet. Detectives were able to determine the date of the photos by analysing the dog's teeth which gave its age – but such analysis required a general anaesthetic from which the dog did not recover. This was said to be the only occasion when Hindley showed emotion.

The death sentence in Great Britain had been overturned when Ian Brady and Myra Hindley were arrested, so, in May 1966, Brady was sentenced to three terms of life imprisonment (for three murders) and Hindley two terms plus seven years for harbouring Brady.

VARIETY IN NOTORIETY

Jack the Stripper was an unknown serial killer who murdered at least six prostitutes, their nude bodies discovered around the London area between 1964 and 1965. The Krays' associate, Freddie Mills, former world light-heavyweight champion, was suspected of these murders but was found shot dead in his car in Soho in July 1965, his death written off as suicide.

Kenneth Halliwell took an overdose in August 1967 after smashing in Joe Orton's skull with a hammer. The ashes of the gay couple (Orton, of course, famous for such plays as *Entertaining Mr Sloane* and *Loot*) were mixed together with the reluctant permission of Orton's brother, Douglas.

When Mary Bell was convicted of murdering two young boys in 1968, there was a problem as to what to do with her as she was just 11 years old. Mental institutions at the time did not seem appropriate, prison was obviously out of the question, and institutes for 'troubled' children would have had problems. The solution: a high-security boys' reform school. An interesting choice with puberty on the horizon.

Another unknown serial killer picked up at least three victims at the Barrowland Ballroom in Glasgow in the 1960s – over 100 policemen worked on the case and 50,000 statements were taken, to no avail. In spite of a description, over 250 identity parades drew a blank. He was known as Bible John because he was believed to quote the scriptures to his victims.

When three policemen were shot dead near Wormwood Scrubs in 1966, it sparked one of the biggest manhunts in British criminal history. One eye-witness had been canny enough to note the registration number of the car containing the criminals, meaning the owner, John Witney, was picked up within hours. John Duddy, another of the three men responsible, was picked up a few days later in Scotland, but it took three months to find the last – Harry Roberts. Police had even searched Sadler's Wells Theatre during a performance of the opera *Bluebeard* following up one tip-off, but he was found somewhere far less glamorous: in a hideout made of tarpaulin covered with used fertiliser bags painted green and black, in a rural part of Essex. This hideout was subsequently auctioned with the proceeds given to a police fund! Not surprisingly, all three men received life sentences.

The term Rachmanism lives on as a result of Peter Rachman charging extortionate rents for London slums, mainly around Notting Hill, in the early 1960s, while at the same time managing to avoid paying a penny in tax. Something he did not achieve, however, which his predominantly West Indian tenants managed, was British Citizenship – he was Polish. Because of libel laws, Rachman's name and his property racketeering were not widely known until after his 1962 death – when some comedian joked that if you opened his grave, you would probably find a couple of tenants inside.

CRIMES WITH A DIFFERENCE

When Sarah Harvey was sentenced to 15 months in prison in 1960 for obtaining £2 per week by deception, she had managed to avoid a murder charge. Her son had discovered the mummified body of her former lodger, Mrs Knight, when prising open a locked cupboard door at his mother's home when she was in hospital. (That taught him what curiosity did.) Sarah Harvey had been collecting the 'invalid' Mrs Knight's 'support money' from the clerk of the magistrates' court in Rhyl – for twenty years. Although there was a ligature around the mummified body, the timing of the death made it impossible to secure a conviction against Mrs Harvey, who claimed she had panicked when she found her lodger dead, and stashed her in the cupboard, collecting the money to avoid a false accusation of murder.

Bearded actor Toneye [*sic*] Manning was jailed at Brixton in February 1968 for contempt of court when he refused to return Arthur the cat to Spillers. Arthur was the white, feline star of the Kattomeat advertisements on television, who fed himself from a can. Manning claimed that it was his cat that he had loaned to Spillers, but they maintained they had bought the cat for £700. He had tried to avoid jail by spinning an interesting yarn suggesting that Arthur was in the custody of the Soviet Embassy and thus 'out of his hands'. Not only an actor but a fantasist, it seems.

SOME SIXTIES SPIES (EXCLUDING JAMES BOND)

Kim Philby – awarded Soviet citizenship as a reward for his services to Russia in July 1963, after fleeing the UK disguised as an Arab. He admitted to spying for the Soviets for some thirty years.

Englishman Greville Wynne was tried in Moscow in May 1963 and was sentenced to three years in prison and five in a labour camp (his Russian associate, Oleg Penkovsky, was sentenced to death).

However, Wynne was exchanged for Gordon Lonsdale in 1964, a professional spy from the Soviet Union (real name Kolon/Konon Molodi/Molody) who had been running a company selling juke boxes and bubble gum machines in the UK – not quite as lucrative as spying.

Double agent George Blake escaped from the maximum security wing at Wormwood Scrubs in October 1966 after serving only four years of his record-breaking 42-year sentence. The ladder he used was made of knitting needles, smuggled in by a released prisoner, along with a carjack to bend the cell bars, and wire cutters. (Yep, maximum security). In Moscow, he received the Order of Lenin.

A prison riot at Parkhurst, Isle of Wight, in October 1969 was prompted by the early release of Russian spy Peter Kroger who had been arrested with Lonsdale in 1961, forming part of the so-called Portland Spy Ring. Fifty people were injured in the fracas. Kroger and his wife (real surname Cohen) were exchanged with British spy Gerald Brooke who had been incarcerated in a Soviet prison, and were hailed as heroes in Russia, their images appearing on a postage stamp.

Minor Admiralty civil servant William Vassall was arrested on suspicion of spying for the Russians in 1962, ending up with a sentence of 18 years. He had given himself away by living beyond his means with holidays in Capri and Egypt (when everyone else went to Clacton or Brighton), his expensive wardrobe, and his even more expensive flat in Dolphin Square in central London.

And a 'retired' spy . . .

In 1964, an American who had been at Cambridge with Anthony Blunt, told FBI and MI-5 agents that Blunt (a retired member of the British Intelligence Service) had tried to recruit him to spy for the Soviet Union. Exposed as a member of the Cambridge spy ring, Blunt provided information regarding his past operations and his associates, most of whom had died or defected to Russia, out of reach of British prosecutors. In exchange, Blunt was not tried for his offences and continued his new career in art history. (His Cambridge spy ring colleagues from the 1950s were Guy Burgess and Donald Maclean who defected to the USSR during that decade).

HEADLINES RE MODS AND ROCKERS CLASHES AT CLACTON, EASTER 1964

Youngsters Beat Up Town
Wild Ones Invade Seaside
Sawdust Caesars
Day of Terror by Scooter Groups

But these were just the headlines. In fact, although there were 97 arrests, plus 76 in Brighton and 51 in Margate a few weeks later (May), only a tenth were charged with offences involving violence. A few were charged with such offences as 'obtaining credit to the amount of 7*d* by means of fraud' – i.e. stealing an ice-cream. Other interesting newspaper reports made such claims as 'all dance halls near sea front smashed' (in Clacton) but the town only had one dance hall, which suffered some broken windows, or 'boats overturned' when in fact one boat had overturned. Nothing changes when it comes to newspaper reporting.

MEANWHILE, ON THE OTHER SIDE OF THE POND

In 1962, three prisoners escaped from maximum security prison Alcatraz, on the island in San Francisco Bay, using spoons and a home-made raft. They were never recaptured, but whether they escaped or drowned is a matter of conjecture. Inmates had included Al Capone and Robert 'The Birdman' Stroud, but this episode was the beginning of the end for the famous prison, which was proving too expensive to run. It was finally closed in March 1963 – and became a home for native Americans, briefly, from 1969. A film about the escape was made in the 1970s, starring Clint Eastwood.

When James French was executed in the USA in 1966, he told a reporter that he had a great idea for a headline: 'French Fries'.

The Hippie Utopia went horribly wrong when Sharon Tate (Mrs Roman Polanski) was murdered by chilled out Charles Manson in August 1969. He and his family may have practised free love and soft drugs, but the outcome became one of the most high-profile

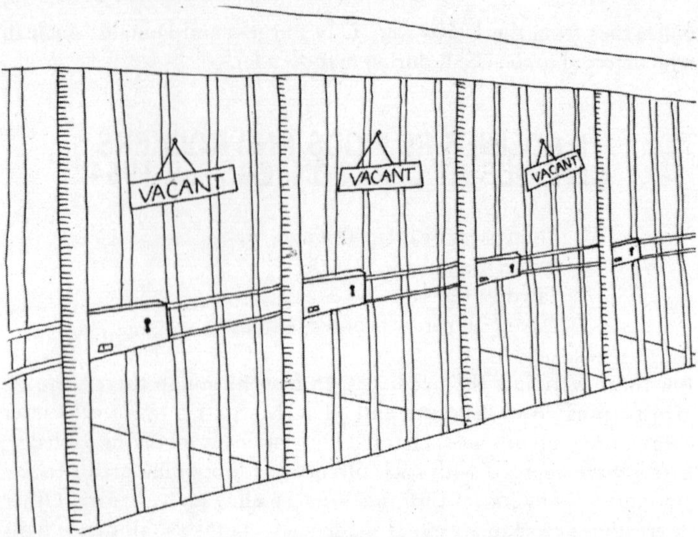

murder cases of the 1960s, even of the twentieth century. Actor Steve McQueen, incidentally, was invited to the party that became the venue for murder, but opted out at the last minute.

Before their double hanging in Kansas in 1965, Perry Smith and Richard Hickock ordered garlic bread, shrimp, French fries, ice cream, strawberries and whipped cream as their last meal. For some strange reason, however, they lost their appetites and left the food untouched!

The Boston Strangler is said to have strangled thirteen women between 1962 and 1964, but the man imprisoned – Albert de Salvo – may not have been responsible for all of these deaths. As he was killed in prison in 1973, the truth died with him.

The 'last request' made by Utah murderer James W. Rodgers before facing the firing squad in 1960 was for a bulletproof vest.

ASSASSINATIONS IN THE US IN THE SIXTIES WERE UNPRECEDENTED

President John Kennedy was shot and killed on 22 November 1963 – sharing common ground with Abraham Lincoln a century earlier. Both presidents were shot on a Friday, in public view, seated next to their wives, after being warned to avoid the area in question, and both were succeeded by a Southerner named Johnson.

Lee Harvey Oswald, alleged murderer of JFK, was shot in front of television cameras by strip-club owner Jack Ruby on 24 November 1963 in the underground car park of the Dallas Police HQ.

Malcolm X, the black Muslim leader, was killed in New York in 1965.

Dr Martin Luther King was murdered in April 1968 – his assassin, James Earl Ray, was arrested in London two months later.

Robert Kennedy was shot in June 1968 while campaigning for the presidency.

AND THERE'S MORE . . .

In Bolivia – while trying to organise a revolt, Che Guevara was captured and killed in October 1967 after 'falling out' with Fidel Castro. A post-mortem examination two days after his death suggested he had not been killed in battle but had been executed.

In Germany – from 1966, Rudolf Hess (Hitler's deputy) became the only prisoner left in Spandau Prison.

In South Africa – Nelson Mandela, anti-apartheid campaigner, was sentenced to life imprisonment on 14 June 1964 for sabotage. He spent most of his time serving hard labour in Robben Island prison off Cape Town. This followed the notorious Sharpeville Massacre of 1960 when police shot and killed more than 50 peaceful anti-apartheid demonstrators, injuring more than 100.

In Israel – Adolf Eichmann was executed on 31 May 1962 for war crimes.

In London – on 18 February 1961 some 5,000 protestors joined a sit-down protest against nuclear testing at the Ministry of Defence in Whitehall. Philosopher-author-aristocrat Sir Bertrand Russell and his wife both served one week in jail for their part (commuted from the original two months' sentence – after all, he was 89). This was one of many such protests organised mainly by CND during this period.

In Northern Ireland – the 'troubles' began with the rise of the Civil Rights Movement in the mid-1960s. Violence erupted in 1966 following the twin 50th anniversaries of the Battle of the Somme and the Easter Rising – respective touchstones for Protestants and Catholics.

In Italy – actress Sophia Loren was tried for complicity in bigamy in Rome in 1962, following her marriage to Carlo Ponti whose previous marriage was considered still valid. The result was the annulment of their marriage, but they became French citizens and remarried in France in 1966.

And, lastly, at Heathrow – so many robberies involving gems, currency and bullion took place in the 1960s that the airport became known as 'Thief Row'.

4

FOOD & DRINK

A DOZEN NEW FOOD EXPERIENCES

Instant mashed potato arrived in the UK with Yeoman from Mars and Smash from Cadbury.

Plastic-wrapped white sandwich loaves arrived in 1961 via Chorleywood Flour Milling, thanks to a demand for soft, springy white bread that didn't go stale quickly. A bonus was the uniformity of the slices. By 1969, 42,000,000 were sold every week in Britain.

Nescafé instant coffee started moving from tins to glass jars in 1961, starting with brown glass.

Batchelor's Vesta curries were launched in 1961. These could be described as the first TV dinners.

Pesto arrived in delicatessens, although it stayed undiscovered on the shelves for a number of years.

PG Tips introduced tea bags, but these also took a number of years to catch on.

Gold Blend, the first freeze-dried instant coffee in the UK, was introduced by Nescafé in 1965.

Cheese and onion crisps were launched by Golden Wonder in 1962, with smoky bacon in 1964, roast chicken in 1967 and beef and onion in 1969.

Hellmann's mayonnaise arrived from the US in 1961, with mayonnaise a new experience for Brits.

Chilled, rather than frozen, chicken was introduced by Marks and Spencer by the end of the decade.

Bovril introduced their instant beef stock in 1966.

Chicken tikka masala was apparently 'invented' in Glasgow during the 1960s when gravy was added to chicken tandoori (made with tomato soup, cream and spices). CTM is now a British favourite.

Mr Kipling cakes were introduced in 1967.

EATING OUT – THE CHOICES

The Ace Café on the North Circular or the Busy Bee on the Watford bypass were the haunt of Rockers and bikers, with rock 'n' roll blasting out of the juke-boxes, a mug of tea, egg and chips, and then a run to the coast. The Busy Bee featured in *Alfie*, and the Ace in *The Leather Boys*, iconic 1960s films. They closed in 1967 and 1969 respectively, partly due to revamped motorway networks (although the Ace has since been revitalised).

OR there was the restaurant that Robert Carrier opened in Camden Passage, Islington, in 1966. The ambience was French, as was much of the food – terrines and crêpes suzette for example. Carrier became better known as a cookery writer and his *Great Dishes of the World* (1967) became a classic of the genre which has sold in its millions. He was also canny enough to open a specialised cookery department in Harrods in 1967 – an outlet for his books and his innovative cookery cards, the latter featuring such recipes as sardine-stuffed lemons.

OR the Berni Inn, which is reputed to have opened a new branch every month in the 1960s to cater for the increasing number of people eating out. Aberdeen Angus Steak Houses (sometimes known just as Angus Steak Houses), also dating from the 1960s in London, offered similar fare.

OR Le Gavroche which opened in 1967 in Sloane Street, London, destined to become Britain's first Michelin-starred restaurant. The Roux brothers were the chefs behind the world-class French cuisine.

OR The Sizzling Sausage and/or Chips with Everything, destined as a chain of restaurants for the young market, financed by J. Lyons & Co. Interesting idea – but it didn't take off in the same way that the Lyons' Corner Houses had in earlier decades.

OR Seed, which opened in 1968 in the basement of the Gloucester Hotel, London. This was one of the first macrobiotic restaurants in the city, but offering more than just rice rissoles and falafel. The organic vegetables, authentic laver bread, vegetable tempura and seaweed dishes attracted the likes of John Lennon and Yoko Ono, as did the psychedelic background music.

OR The Golden Egg, another 1960s chain. This one specialised in fry-ups but in a very new atmosphere of outlandish colour schemes and bright lights.

OR Leith's, in Kensington Park Road, London, although Prue Leith did not open this until 1969 (she set up a successful catering company first, supplying business lunches). This became popular from the off because, according to Prue herself, they used fresh, not canned or frozen, produce – and because the competition was so poor.

OR take your pick of the hundreds of new trattorias and Indian restaurants that opened in the 1960s thanks to the newly acquired taste for 'foreign' foods. In 1960, you could count the number of Indian restaurants in Britain on your fingers, but there were well over 1,000 by the end of the decade. Chinese restaurants were already popular and established by the 1960s but also grew in number.

THE LASTING FACE OF FAST FOOD

When Pizza Express opened its first restaurant in Wardour Street, London, in 1965, the first day's takings were £3. But Brits eventually acquired a taste for travel, and pizza, and the rest really is history.

Wimpy Bars (which started out in the 1950s) were opening at the rate of one every week by the late 1960s, with 461 open by 1969. (McDonalds and Burger King did not arrive in the UK until the 1970s.)

The first British branch of Kentucky Fried Chicken opened in Preston in 1965 and was an immediate hit with the locals.

NOVEL CONFECTIONERY

After Eight Mints were introduced in 1962, with other sweet treats to follow:

Topic in 1962

Toffee Crisp in 1963

Jelly Tots in 1965

Twix in 1967

Marathon in 1967

Matchmakers in 1968

WHEN EVEN ICE LOLLIES WERE BASED ON POPULAR CULTURE

Zoom was introduced in 1963 shaped like a rocket in keeping with the *Fireball XL5* TV series, and Sea Jet soon followed – based on *Stingray*. In 1963, Pick of the Pops arrived with a rather more sophisticated feel, coated in chocolate and with coffee and advocaat flavours. Fab, another ice lolly, was launched in 1967, based on *Thunderbirds* with Smash similarly advertised two years later. Orbit (1968) was similar to Zoom, though based on *Captain Scarlet and the Mysterons* and using appropriate orange and chocolate colours/flavours. Promotional material for Luv in 1969, aimed at the girls, included collectable pictures of pop stars.

CELEBRITY CHEFS ARE NOTHING NEW

Following on from the first celebrity chef, Philip Harben in the 1950s, the best-known 1960s chefs were female:

Fanny Cradock was renowned for wearing ball-gowns, false eyelashes, tiaras and the like for her TV demonstrations. Her excesses extended to her food, with brandy and cream piled into just about every recipe, and a penchant for the unlikely. Recipes included kidneys flambéed in brandy, Green Cheese ice-cream (with food dye added), blue-dyed boiled eggs, duchesse potatoes (also dyed green), and the prawn cocktail which she claimed to have invented. Eccentric and inaccurate in her views (Christmas was 'pagan'; Chinese restaurants won't last; couscous parties will be the 'in-thing'), she was also renowned for the way she berated and humiliated her apparently downtrodden fourth husband-to-be, Johnnie, on camera. They don't make them like that anymore.

Marguerite Patten first appeared on a TV cookery show in 1947 and was cooking for a BBC TV programme called *Designed for Women* until the early 1960s. She was also President of their Cookery Club until 1961, testing viewers' recipes. Marguerite was one of the first cookery experts to embrace the idea of new imported tastes such as garlic, fondue, olive oil and snails. Her 1960 cook book *Cookery in Colour* sold several million copies.

Elizabeth David became the leading food writer during the decade, hell-bent on transforming English menus. She had a column in the *Spectator*, and many of her books were released as Penguin paperbacks. Like Fanny Cradock, she had a rather turbulent private life, starting out as an actress; and she held similarly strong views on most things food-related – 'Why crispy not crisp?' and 'Why Welsh rarebit not Welsh rabbit?' and 'Garlic presses are useless'. In 1966, she opened her own cookware shop in Pimlico, London – which did not stock garlic presses. She became renowned not only for her books but for such new kitchen equipment as English iron pans, tin moulds, unadorned crockery and French coffee cups.

NOT FORGETTING . . .

Delia Smith started as a waitress at the Singing Chef in Paddington, London, in the 1960s, and wrote her first piece for the *Daily Mirror* in 1969 featuring kipper pâté and beef in beer. 1969 was also the year she was asked to produce an 'over-the-top and gaudy' cake for the cover of the Rolling Stones' album, 'Let It Bleed'.

Graham Kerr, known as the Galloping Gourmet has not been overlooked, but wasn't really established in the UK until the very end of the 1960s. He was far more popular in Canada and Australia.

GO TO WORK ON AN EGG

This was an advertising campaign (which ran from 1957 to 1971) featuring such well-known names as Tony Hancock and Patricia Hayes. It was responsible in part for the peak in egg consumption in the UK during the 1960s – reaching five eggs per person per week.

One person who took note was the Chancellor of the Exchequer, Derick Heathcoat-Amory, who collapsed in 1960 while delivering a budget – confessing that he had eaten nothing but a poached egg 'for days'.

TEN FOOD & DRINK PRICES

In 'old money' of course!
2 frozen fish steaks (from Eskimo) 1*s* 10*d* (1960)
Loaf of bread 1*s* (1961)
Sliced loaf 1*s* 8*d* (1969)
1lb New Zealand Butter 3*s* 11*d* (1960)
49*s* 11*d* for a bottle of Scotch (1969)
2*s* 3*d* for ½lb Golden Meadow butter (1969)
1*s* for a large tin of Heinz baked beans (1969)
7*s* 11*d* for 8oz jar of Nescafé coffee (1969)
Chilled chicken 2*s* 6*d* per lb (1969)
10*d* for a packet of Jacob's Cream Crackers (1969)

If you need help converting that: *s*, a shilling = 5p;
d, a penny = less than 0.5p nowadays.

GREEN SHIELD STAMPS

These could be collected from a number of supermarkets and garages, with one stamp for each 6*d* spent. In 1963, Tesco became one of the largest providers of Green Shield Stamps (long before the Tesco Clubcard). The stamps were stuck in a book and saved for a range of gifts chosen from the Green Shield catalogue. You would need to spend £32 (far more than the average weekly wage in the mid-1960s) to fill just one book for which you could get such essentials as a mouth organ, a cigarette box or some salad servers. For just over thirteen books, you could get a Kodak Brownie camera, but you needed over 30 books for a Kenwood Chef food mixer and a staggering 88 of them for a 19in television. A new form of philately.

THE SUPERMARKET SPREAD

When Lord Privy Seal Ted Heath abandoned the retail price maintenance scheme in 1961 – at the suggestion of a certain Mr Cohen (of Tesco fame) – it opened the door to low prices for the bulk buyers but had an adverse effect on the independent stores. The 1960s became the decade of the supermarket with a variety of sources giving a figure of 3,400 such stores in the UK by 1969.

Asda opened its first supermarket in 1965, and the first stores were in Yorkshire, utilising converted cinemas. The name comes from ASquith DAiries, its earliest trade name.

Tesco in Leicester opened in 1961 and entered the *Guinness Book of Records* as the largest store in Europe. The first Tesco Superstore opened in Crawley in 1968. (Note that the Tesco name in fact dates from long before the Second World War – 1924 to be precise).

Another established trader, Sainsburys, became the first food retailer to computerise its distribution in 1961.

Bejam was founded in 1968, when frozen food was still in its infancy in Britain. The name comes from the original directors, Brian, Eric, John and Millie – not a lot of people know that. It's now known as Iceland.

Safeway opened its first store in Bedford in 1962. It eventually merged into Morrison's.

However, there was also a growth in health food shops and natural food stores during the 1960s – perhaps to offset the very idea of supermarket shopping.

THREE B'S

The Birds Eye company took on a majority stake in a fishing company in 1965 to secure a regular supply of cod. Unfortunately, a drop in world fish prices followed (allied to operating problems) and they sold the assets just four years later. Slippery to pin down, cod.

The Bovril company had grown to such an extent by 1968 that it owned beef ranches in Argentina said to be half the size of England!

Its 1960 poster boy was teenage football prodigy Jimmy Greaves, and its slogan was 'Drink your health in Bovril'. (If only he had).

Billy Butlin may not be associated with catering as such but in 1966 he won the catering contract for the revolving restaurant at the top of the GPO Tower in London's West End. This would need a very different approach to the mass catering of the holiday camps, which involved (in the 1960s) the annual purchase of 100 tons of sausages, 120,000 gallons of soup, over 1,500 tons of potatoes, 240 tons of pork chops and 3.5 million eggs.

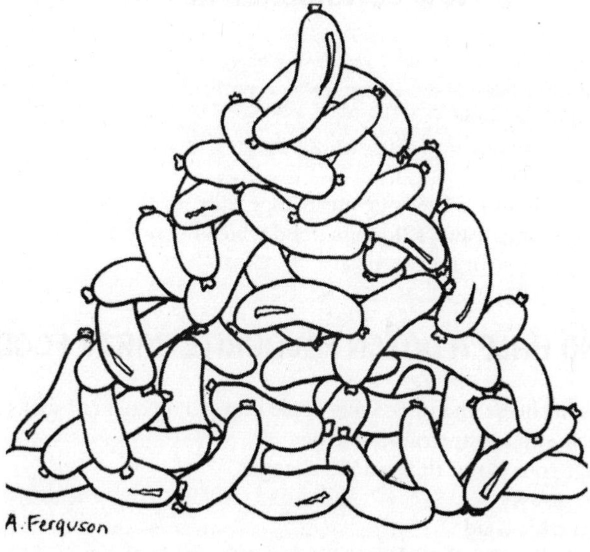

ONE MAN'S VIEW OF PROTEIN

In 1968, Stanley Green launched a campaign which was to last for 25 years. Every day he would cycle from his council flat in Northolt to Oxford Street in London and walk the street with his home-made sandwich board proclaiming:

LESS LUST, BY LESS PROTEIN
LESS FISH, BIRD, MEAT, CHEESE, EGG, BEANS, PEAS, NUTS AND SITTING
[*sic*]

He handed out leaflets produced on his own press, in the belief that protein made people aggressive, and that if its intake was restricted, and a less sedentary lifestyle was introduced, the sexual appetite of the youth of the decade would be radically curbed. His own diet was said to be made up of barley water, porridge, dates, root vegetables, home-made bread and the occasional egg – but where was his scientific evidence? Stanley didn't concern himself with proof, and even though his view didn't catch on, he became rather famous.

EIGHT FAVOURITE FOODS NOW CONSIDERED RETRO

Spam fritters
Jam sandwiches
Bread and dripping
Tripe and onions
Carnation milk
Prawn cocktail – a 1960s favourite especially for the posh
Black Forest gâteau – a 'foreign' food which became a classic
Pigs' trotters – for the less posh

AND HALF A DOZEN FAVOURITE PARTY FOODS

Cubes of cheese and tinned pineapple impaled on cocktail sticks and stuck into a grapefruit or melon
Sausage rolls (some things don't change)
Cheese straws
Tinned fruit salad
Sherry trifle
Angels (or Devils) on horseback – bacon wrapped around oysters or prunes – strictly for the extra-posh

CHEESE CHAT

No less than three bodies were involved in the origins of the Ploughman's Lunch in the 1960s. The English County Cheese Council, the British Milk Marketing Board, and the Licensed Victuallers' Association. The Ploughman's Lunch was a way of promoting the sale of cheese through public houses, with Cheddar becoming the standard ingredient.

In 1960, a professor named Henry Lardy from the University of Wisconsin announced that cigarette filters made with cheese (especially Parmesan or Romano) and charcoal served to remove over 90 per cent of harmful tars. The idea did not catch on.

By the 1960s there were no farmhouse cheesemakers left in the Dales – although there had been over 430 before the Second World War.

In 1960, more than 40,000 tons of Cheshire cheese was produced, but this high has not been maintained.

This British decline in cheesemaking did not deter everyone: the First Milk Cheese Company's creamery in Haverfordwest began cheese production in the 1960s, and Galbani Dolcelatte launched their mild, creamy Italian blue cheese suitable for vegetarians which became their flagship product in the UK. Blue Castello, a Brie-like cheese with a spicy flavour was first developed in the 1960s, and Philadelphia cream cheese appeared in the UK in 1960.

AND NOT – HIC – FORGETTING THE ALCOHOL

The most popular drink was beer (bitter and light ale), with lager gaining popularity. Best-selling brand names included the established Watney's Red Barrel and Bass Red Triangle. New kids on the block were Worthington White Shield IPA also from Bass and the pioneering canned ale by Ind Coope (Long Life). A pint of beer in the mid-1960s, incidentally, would set you back about 1*s* 8*d*. In 1968, Whitbread gained the right to brew Heineken in the UK under a 35-year licence, producing a weaker version which was hugely successful.

For the ladies there were sweet French white wines or, from Portugal, Mateus Rose in the flask-shaped bottle you could make into a table lamp. A British alternative was Babycham from Somerset, launched in the 1950s and becoming iconic in the 1960s, once it started using its baby fawn image. It could be mixed with brandy for the adventurous. Then there was the on-trend 'snowball' – a mixture of advocaat and lemonade. Rum and coke or vodka and lime were gaining in popularity in the pubs and clubs frequented by the young set.

A DRINKERS' TIMELINE

1961 – The Coca Cola company introduced Sprite (followed a few years later by Tab, its first diet drink, and then Fresca).

1962 – Prince Charles was in trouble for drinking Cherry Brandy when he was aged 14 while out for a meal with pupils from Gordonstoun School.

1964 – *Blue Peter* (the television programme) was similarly censured – over a ginger pop recipe described by the Temperance Union as a 'dangerously alcoholic brew'.

1965 – Tennents's beer cans featured a series of twenty women, each can with a different beer-related recipe. This was the Housewives' Choice collection intended to woo the female drinker.

1965 – The first boxed wine was invented and patented in Australia.

1965 – Statistics for wine-drinking that year revealed that UK drinkers sank 9.2 pints of wine, compared to 189.2 in Italy, so the Brits had a lot of catching up to do.

1968 – Watney's introduced the Party 7 can, following the success of their Party 4. For serious drinkers.

1969 – Coca Cola's new slogan (following an earlier trial) was 'It's the Real Thing'.

1969 – Schweppes (the carbonated drinks company) merged with Cadbury becoming, imaginatively, Cadbury Schweppes.

1969 – *The Guinness Book of Records* lists the speed drinking record as having been set by a 20-year-old known as 'The Broom', who drunk a 2.5 pint yard of ale in 6.5 seconds.

THE LAST WORD ON DRINK – WELL, WATER ACTUALLY

In the *Liverpool Echo* in March 1961, there was a quote from the Lord Mayor's speech regarding the new fluoridation programme being introduced. It included the immortal injunction:

'Let Liverpool . . . give a national lead to other great cities . . . What Liverpool drinks today, the rest of the country drinks tomorrow.'

. . . Think about it.

5

FILM & TELEVISION (AND NOT FORGETTING RADIO)

THE STORIES BEHIND SOME FAMOUS FILMS

Antonioni's first English language film was the first British feature film to show full-frontal female nudity – this was *Blow-Up* in 1966, loosely based on the exploits of Swingin' London photographers David Bailey and Terence Donovan. The naked lady was the little-known Jane Birkin. In one of the club scenes, the eagle-eyed can spot Janet Street-Porter – but she was fully clothed, in striped PVC trousers – dancing to a Yardbirds track. Although starring David Hemmings and Vanessa Redgrave, the resident diva – or divo – was in fact Antonioni who had hampers from Fortnum & Mason every lunchtime, and a white Rolls-Royce to bring him to the set every day. He was also unhappy with the colours of the grass and trees at South London's Maryon Park and had them repainted in more acceptable shades of green and brown respectively.

The 'asides' to the audience that featured so prominently in *Alfie* (1966) were not quite as revolutionary as advertised at the time – *Tom Jones*, three years earlier (starring Albert Finney and Susannah York), had made use of the ploy. Incidentally, one of the actors to turn down the part – mainly because of the inclusion of the abortion scene – was Michael Caine's room-mate, Terence Stamp, who had played the part on stage (presumably with no such scene). Caine went on to win a Golden Globe and an Oscar nomination for his performance as the swaggering chauvinist.

An early example of ageism was the replacement of Dorothy Lamour with Joan Collins when the first *Road* film after a ten-year absence was produced in 1962 – *The Road to Hong Kong*. Bing Crosby and Bob Hope featured as prominently as ever, but Dorothy was offered a small walk-on part, which she only accepted after it was enlarged. The filming was at Shepperton, with a plot influenced by that decade's new interest in space travel.

British actor/producer Stanley Baker opened a whole can of worms when he took on the filming of *Zulu* in South Africa, the film that brought Michael Caine international recognition upon its release in 1964. The Zulus he'd hired (some 700 of them) had for the most part not even seen a film, so Baker arranged for them to see a Western before filming started. At this stage, he had also decided he wanted Roy Kinnear for one part, but couldn't remember his name and asked for 'the actor in *That Was the Week That Was* whose surname begins with K' – one David Kernan (also in *TW3*) turned up, so Baker took him on anyway. After filming, the Zulus were not allowed to attend the premier because of apartheid laws, nor were they allowed to be paid the same as white actors. The latter problem was solved in an original fashion – by gifting the animals purchased for the movie (including a number of cows) to the actors to make up the difference!

When London-born Alfred Hitchcock bought the screen rights to Robert Bloch's novel *Psycho* (amazingly for less than $9,000) he is also said to have bought up as many copies of the novel as he could to keep the ending a secret. The stabbing scene in the shower took seven days to shoot, but only lasts 45 seconds, and the music, by Bernard Hermann, was so successful that he apparently had his salary doubled by an originally sceptical Hitchcock. When the film – the first to 'feature' a flushing toilet! – was released in 1960, Hitchcock issued contracts to cinemas insisting on no admission after the film had begun – when one cinema manager phoned to complain on behalf of disgruntled customers waiting in the rain, Hitchcock's response was 'Buy them umbrellas.' The *Psycho* house, incidentally, or rather the set, turns up in a number of other films and television productions, e.g. *Wagon Train*.

The British, and Quaker, film-maker David Lean claimed that all the movement in his smash hit of 1962, *Lawrence of Arabia*, was intentionally left to right to emphasise the journey involved. Peter O'Toole, rather less pretentiously, claimed that during the making of this film he constantly referred to Omar Sharif as Fred because 'no one' is called 'Omar Sharif'! At 227 minutes, this has been logged as the longest film without a woman in a speaking role (early days, ladies), and is additionally remarkable for the number of 'real' soldiers used in the casting – many of which were loaned by King Hussein of Jordan.

In 1966, the third of Clint Eastwood's Spaghetti Westerns was one of the year's biggest box office successes. It was *The Good, The Bad and The Ugly* – which had no dialogue for the opening ten and a half minutes. The iconic poncho associated with Clint Eastwood in the films was only worn for the last seventeen minutes in this, the final of the trilogy, suggesting it should perhaps have been the first of the three as the poncho was worn rather more in the earlier movies. Something to think about . . . but not for long.

The first Bond film, 1962's *Dr No*, made a real emphasis on its Britishness with Savile Row suits, the snobbery of the wine class and the martini-shaken-not-stirred brigade. In spite of this, it was an international success, of course, with Japan's translation (literally) one of the more interesting: 'We Don't Want a Doctor'. Sean Connery, however, was reputedly paid only £5,000 for the role.

During the making of *Doctor Dolittle* (a 1967 film), the ducks were turned loose on a pond – but promptly sank because they had lost their waterproof feathers: it was the moulting season. Who said 'Shoot the researcher?' Not only that, but squirrels ate the scenery, goats ate the scripts, and Rex Harrison, the lead, was either urinated on or bitten on more than one occasion by a whole range of animals – not one of his happier experiences. It not only resulted in a dramatic downturn for his career, but lost 20th Century Fox a fortune at the box office. This was fame of a very different kind.

Hollywood blockbuster *Cleopatra* (1963) featured more than three British stars (i.e. Taylor and Burton, and not forgetting Rex Harrison on happier form as Caesar) – there was George Cole as Flavius, for a start, and roles for such as Richard O'Sullivan, Michael Hordern, Francesca Annis, Michael Gwynn, Kenneth Haigh, Gwen Watford and an uncredited John Alderton. As for the role of Mark Antony, this could have been played by an Irishman rather than a Welshman if Stephen Boyd had been able to accept the role. Liz Taylor became the first star to receive a $1million for her performance, and Eddie Fisher (her then husband) had what could have been the embarrassing task of ensuring she was awake on time in the mornings – for which he was reputedly paid £1,000 per day. Incidentally, the finished film was banned in, of all places, Egypt – because Liz was a Jewish convert. While the producers did not do much in the way of economising, including spending a lavish $195,000 on Cleo's costumes alone, at least the abandoned sets used in London were reused for *Carry on Cleo* in 1964, and Richard Burton's outfits were reused by Sid James. Interesting to note that this latter film sparked the possibility of legal action when Marks and Spencer took, temporary, aversion to the use of Marcus and Spencius in the story although these were the names of, er, slave traders.

OSCAR WINNERS – BEST FILM

An American award, but note the British influence that crept in:

1960 *Ben Hur* – Brits Stephen Boyd and Jack Hawkins feature prominently, along with Hugh Griffith and Finlay Currie – note the 'full monty': an Irishman, Englishman, Welshman and Scotsman. There was also an uncredited John Le Mesurier, later of *Dad's Army*.

1961 *The Apartment* – sadly, we cannot take any credit here.
1962 *West Side Story* – one name – William Shakespeare!
1963 *Lawrence of Arabia* – the David Lean epic.
1964 *Tom Jones* – at £500,000, one of the most expensive British films ever made – at the time.
1965 *My Fair Lady* – the most expensive musical ever made, featuring the stalwart Rex Harrison with Wilfrid Hyde-White and Stanley Holloway – it doesn't come much more British than that. The film won Oscars for every possible category, in fact, except Best Actress because Audrey Hepburn could not be nominated as her singing voice was dubbed – could have won this too if British star Julie Andrews had been cast!
1966 *The Sound of Music* – Julie Andrews contributed to this being the biggest box office success of the 1960s . . . bit of a surprise to some.
1967 *A Man for All Seasons* – brought in the heavyweights including Paul Schofield and Vanessa Redgrave, more modestly attired than in 1966; winning six Oscars.
1968 *In the Heat of the Night* – one of only two exceptions.
1969 *Oliver!* – Charles Dickens, Lionel Bart and Ron Moody – what a combination – but missing Jim Davidson, who failed the audition for the Artful Dodger.

MAKING MONEY AT THE BRITISH BOX OFFICE

Although there were a lot of British cinemas turning into bowling alleys in the 1960s, and then into bingo halls, the industry was not full of doom and gloom. Saturday morning pictures at local cinemas up and down the country did well at the beginning of the decade for schoolchildren, and the first triplex cinema in the country opened in Edinburgh at the end of the decade (1969). British cinema-goers did not necessarily agree with the Oscar winners, and the best measure of this is in what films made the most money, so here is a very different list for the 1960s in Britain, attributable to the British Film Institute:

The Sound of Music – £30 million (one of only three Best Film Oscar winners featured)
The Jungle Book – £19.8 million
Thunderball – £15.6 million (the 4th Bond film)
Mary Poppins – £14 million (it's that Julie Andrews again)

Goldfinger – £13.9 million (the third Bond film – with Pussy Galore's pilots actually men in blonde wigs)
The Guns of Navarone – £11.4 million (described at the time as 'Elderly Gang Goes to War')
Doctor Zhivago – £11.2 million (David Lean's most successful film ever)
101 Dalmatians – £9.1 million (made £224 million gross internationally, making it the top-earner – another surprise)
Oliver! – £8.9 million (entirely filmed at Shepperton – even the steam railway)
My Fair Lady – £8.6 million (with Rex Harrison on form, despite the fact that he couldn't sing)

THE SYMBOLIC SIXTIES

Here come the message films:
Doctor Strangelove (1964) satirised nuclear war and exposed the talents of Peter Sellers

Born Free (1966) the start of the ecology crusade and the back-to-nature movement, inspired by London-born Virginia McKenna

The Graduate (1967) was the first memorable coming-of-age film, with Robert Redford declining the Dustin Hoffman role as he lacked the naivety required

Easy Rider (1969) was perhaps the first up-the-establishment film, a new version of the 'road film' and one of the first to use rock music as a soundtrack

And films showing new preoccupations:
2001: A Space Odyssey (1968) and *Barbarella* (1967) with their very different interpretations of the space age – not to mention *Barbarella*'s pre-occupation with sex

A Hard Day's Night (1964), *Help* (1965), *Magical Mystery Tour* (1967) and *Yellow Submarine* (1968) – all vehicles for The Beatles. *A Hard Day's Night* was shot in black and white because its financial backers were not convinced it would become successful! As for *Yellow Submarine*, the Beatles did not supply their own voices – although they did make a cameo appearance at the end of the film

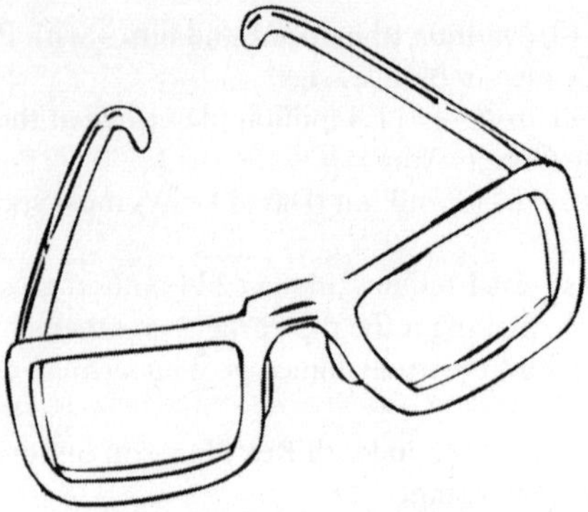

The Ipcress File (1962) – not just because Michael Caine demonstrates the 'new man' by cooking an omelette, but also because it reinforced the public interest in the world of the spy

TALKING OF SPIES

Caine followed up his dour Harry Palmer role with *Funeral in Berlin* (1966) and *Billion Dollar Brain* (1967) – the first 'action hero' with glasses.

Richard Burton played the equally dour lead in John Le Carré's *The Spy Who Came in From the Cold* (1965), true to the novel apart from the change in name of the leading female from Liz (because of the Liz Taylor association) to Nan.

As for the Spy Supremo – the name James Bond was taken from the ornithologist author of one of Ian Fleming's favourite books *Birds of the West Indies* (the feathered kind). In the second Bond outing, *From Russia With Love* (1963), it seems that Sean Connery doubled up in the opening minutes as a SPECTRE agent – wearing a James Bond mask (!) but in fact it is a look-alike extra – confusing. And for the last word on 007, or rather Bond girls, it was good to see that the second Miss UK to win Miss World, Ann Sidney, achieved her ambition to be in a Bond movie in 1967

– with an uncredited appearance in *You Only Live Twice* (a film for which Roald Dahl wrote the screenplay). She was in good company as Connery's wife, Diane Cilento, also went uncredited, appearing as a 'stunt swimming double' according to the Internet Movie Database.

MORE FILM FIRSTS

When Sophia Loren won the Best Actress Oscar in 1962 for *Two Women*, she became the first to do so in a foreign language (Italian) film.

Sidney Poitier became the first black actor to receive an Oscar, in 1964, for *The Lilies of the Field.*

The first use of the F word on screen was in 1967 in a typically swinging sixties London movie, *I'll Never Forget What's'isname* – voiced by Marianne Faithfull.

The first director to make a million dollars for a single film was Mike Nichols, for *The Graduate*, in 1967.

Bonnie and Clyde, also 1967, was the first film to feature squibs — small explosive charges, usually attached to bags of red liquid and fired from inside an actor's clothes to simulate bullet hits. Three of the banks used on location were actually robbed by the real duo.

The first biker film (*The Wild One*, with Marlon Brando, released in the US in 1953) hit the British screens in 1968 after a ban of fourteen years over here.

1969 saw the first X-rated movie – *Midnight Cowboy* – an American film directed by a Brit, John Schlesinger.

THE BIG WORLD OF MOVIES

Thailand – were still making silent films in the 1960s because the Second World War had disrupted their film industry.

California – world famous horse 'actor' Trigger (Roy Rogers' co-star) died in 1965. He was displayed in the Roy Rogers Museum after 88 films and 100 television shows.

Ireland – Siobhan McKenna had crashed into a ditch, a wall and a tree on her first three driving attempts so her insurance precluded her from driving while making *Of Human Bondage* in 1964 at various locations including her native Ireland.

Italy – a version of *Hamlet* was made here in 1968 with the lead immortalised as a gunslinger in the Wild West, *Johnny Hamlet.*

Germany – during filming of *The Great Escape,* the production team had to obtain permission from the German government to shoot in a national forest – and damaged thousands of trees in the process. As compensation, the film company restored 2,000 pine trees after filming.

France – Brigitte Bardot, the 1950s 'sex kitten', pouted her way through fifteen more films in the 1960s (over half of them in French) and found time to marry German millionaire Gunter Sachs in 1966 and record a handful of musical albums.

Japan – held the record right through the 1960s for the number of feature films it produced.

TEN KITCHEN SINK DRAMAS

The first of these (*Look Back in Anger* and *Room at the Top* in 1959) set a precedent which dominated British films in the 1960s:

Saturday Night and Sunday Morning, 1960

*A Taste of Honey,*1961

A Kind of Loving and *The L-Shaped Room,* 1962

This Sporting Life, 1963

The Leather Boys, 1964

Georgy Girl, 1966

Poor Cow, 1967

Up The Junction, 1968

Kes, 1969

COMPETITION FROM THE SMALL SCREEN

The number of cinemas in Britain was down to 1,800 by 1967 (from 4,500 in 1950). In the mid-1960s, more people were buying televisions on hire purchase, or renting them, than any other item, in spite of the fact that they could cost as much as £130 when the average wage was little more than £1,000 per year. Buyers were undeterred by the existence of just two channels (until BBC2 in 1964 – the opening night of which was ruined by a power failure in London, caused by a fire at Battersea Power Station, delaying the launch by 24 hours) with programmes in black and white (until 1967, starting with Wimbledon coverage – all that lovely green grass) that didn't start till midday or early evening! Approaching 10 million licences were issued in 1960, at a cost of £4, increasing to £5 from 1965 and to £11 to include colour transmission by 1969, the year of the first television detector van. Until the end of the decade, viewers were advised not to sit closer than 6ft to a television screen because the cathode-ray tubes then used emitted a low level of ultra-violet radiation!

Programmes made an effort to reflect changes in popular culture throughout the decade, and there was an increasing move towards showing pop and music programmes to cater for the younger set. *Thank Your Lucky Stars* launched in 1961 and is remembered for The Beatles' first national television appearance in January 1963 followed a few months later by the Rolling Stones – and for teenager Janice Nicholls scoring potential hits with 'foive'. This was the commercial answer to the already established BBC's *Juke Box Jury*, but both programmes were axed by the end of the decade. *Ready Steady Go!* – hosted by Queen of the Mods, Cathy McGowan – was first shown in August 1963, and lasted till the Mod era started its own decline at the end of 1966. *Top of the Pops*, which started out on New Year's Day 1964, lasted rather longer! The dance troupe associated with *Top of the Pops*, Pan's

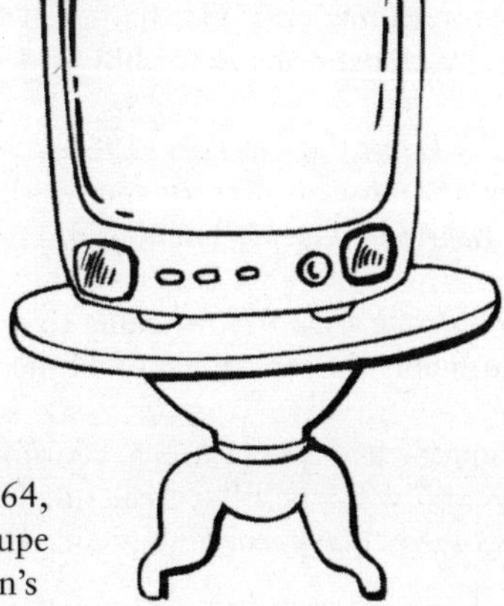

People, did not arrive until 1968, having been preceded by the Gojos. Well over fifty 'music-based' programmes featured during the 1960s, including shows featuring individual singers – everyone from Kathy Kirby (the highest-paid female entertainer at one time, at £1,000 per show) and Billy Fury to Millicent Martin, Russ Conway to Lonnie Donegan.

Even though this up-and-coming form of entertainment had effectively been given the thumbs up by no less than the Duke of Edinburgh – who was interviewed on *Panorama* in 1961 by David Dimbleby – not everyone was happy. Mary Whitehouse collected some 500,000 signatures against 'BBC dirt' in 1965 and formed the National Viewers' and Listeners' Association, a watchdog body. Spoilsport or saviour? You decide.

MEMORABLE SIXTIES TELLY SUCCESSES

Variety

The BBC's *Black and White Minstrel Show* won the first ever Golden Rose in 1961 (for best television show). It also resisted attempts by the Campaign against Racial Discrimination to take it off the air from 1967, holding on for another eleven years, twenty years in all.

Opportunity Knocks (1956–78), a precursor *of Britain's Got Talent* with its technically advanced clap-o-meter (jesting, jesting) to measure applause.

Comedy

Morecambe and Wise had their first successful series in 1961 with ATV, transferring to the BBC in 1968.

Till Death Us Do Part (1966–75) – Warren Mitchell won a BAFTA in 1966 for his performance as the bigoted Alf Garnett (much to the chagrin of Mary Whitehouse).

Hancock's Half Hour came to a premature end mid-1960 but was arguably the forerunner of all sitcoms.

Steptoe and Son (1962–5, returning in the '70s for four more iconic years) was one of several sitcoms (like *Till Death*) starting life in *Comedy Playhouse* and intended as a one-off.

Dad's Army (1968–77) – gave some ageing thespians a second bite of the cherry.

The Likely Lads (1964–6) – filmed in London, not the North-East, despite the accents.

Not Only But Also (1965–70) – reuniting Dudley Moore and Peter Cook from the satirical production, *Beyond the Fringe*, staged a few years earlier.

That Was The Week That Was (or *TW3)* began in November 1962, but only survived (memorably) until December 1963 because of its 'political sensitivity', i.e. an election was on the horizon!

The Dick Emery Show clocked up an amazing 18 years, from 1963, perhaps due to Randy Mandy, or Camp Clarence (with *Benny Hill* following in Dick Emery's footsteps from 1969).

Monty Python only kicked off in 1969, as did *On the Buses* but both – although very different – quickly picked up remarkable viewing figures.

Drama

The Prisoner (just seventeen episodes 1967–8) featured a huge floating white balloon, known as Rover. Incidentally, the voice on the public address system in this series was that of Fenella Fielding, the vampire in *Carry on Screaming*.

Z-Cars (not named after the Ford Zephyr patrol cars – but a reference to Lancaster police call signs) started out in 1962 and ran until 1978, its theme tune adapted by Everton Football Club, presumably because of the perceived Merseyside connection.

The Avengers (1961–9) with John Steed originally assisting Dr David Keel, played by Ian Hendry. Now in the league of 'cult' along with *The Prisoner*.

The Forsyte Saga (from January 1967 on BBC2, repeated BBC1 1968) went against the swinging psychedelic trend of the '60s, winning a BAFTA for best drama series in the process and justifying its tag as the most expensive BBC drama production at that time. It became the last major British drama series to be filmed in black and white and the first to be 'sold' to Russia.

The Saint, which started in black and white in 1962, switched to colour for its next (and last, until the late '70s) four years in 1965.

The Wednesday Play, 1964–70, with its most notable production *Cathy Come Home* (November 1966) watched by half the British population. It brought social issues into everyone's living room – and boosted the profile of new charity, Shelter, for the homeless. *Up the Junction* (1965), dealing with abortion issues, had had a similar effect, and both starred Carol White, directed by Ken Loach.

Soaps

Emergency Ward 10, the first twice-weekly serial, ended its ten-year run in October 1967. In the early days of 'props', it seems that their 1960 mock-up of an iron lung convinced even doctors watching who wrote in to ask where they had got it from! Incidentally, its star, John Alderton, went on to feature in another popular series that ran for three years from 1968: *Please Sir!*

Coronation Street (which could have been called Florizel Street or Jubilee Street) aired December 1960, and had a tremendous impact on the viewing public from the outset. To demonstrate: 83 complaints were received when Ken Barlow said 'bloody' in 1961, the show's first 'expletive'. Many now-famous names cut their teeth, so to speak, in Corrie – among them Richard Beckinsale, Ben Kingsley, Arthur Lowe, Joanna Lumley, Prunella Scales and Martin Shaw.

Compact ran from 1962 to 1965, a possible attempt by the BBC to compete with *Coronation Street.* When the series was dropped, the scriptwriters were already writing . . .

. . . *Crossroads* (1964–88), whose early episodes for ATV were filmed – remarkably and economically, if not always effectively – in one take without editing, and which aired five nights a week.

Game Shows

Double Your Money (1955–68) hosted by Hughie Green and for several years featuring 'cockney' assistant Monica Rose, a 1964 contestant plucked from the audience. Its rival was . . .

. . . *Take Your Pick* (1955–63), the first show in Britain to offer prize money.

University Challenge started out in 1962 (and was resurrected in the '90s after a seven-year break). Its antithesis . . .

. . . *It's a Knockout* aired for the first time in August 1966 and lasted over twenty years. The 1960s episodes were not as manic as later ones as they were pre-Stuart Hall.

What's My Line (1950–67), was popular enough to return in later years.

The Golden Shot (1967–75) with original host Jackie Rae often seeming to forget the rules, and replaced by Bob Monkhouse after just 15 episodes.

American shows

The Fugitive, loosely based on *Les Misérables*, did less well than the musical, running from 1963 for four years, although Dr Kimble did well to survive eight gunshots and four stabbings.

Another doctor, *Dr Kildare*, ran (though less literally) from 1961–6.

Bonanza was a popular series in Britain from 1960, closely followed by other American Westerns in the '60s such as *Laramie, Wagon Train, Rawhide, Cheyenne, Gunsmoke, Maverick, The Virginian* – cowboy fans were spoiled for choice.

Peyton Place (1964–9) was America's first prime-time 'soap' and made stars of Ryan O'Neal and Mia Farrow.

Hawaii Five-O (1968–80), the home of exotic locations in the 50th state, hence Five-O.

And, in a class of its own, *Dr Who* debuted in 1963 with William Hartnell and then Patrick Troughton its 1960s incarnations. The original Daleks sported mechanical grabs made out of sink plungers. Those were the days.

THIRTEEN MORE STARTERS . . .

Some familiar names here – *Candid Camera* first broadcast in 1960; *Songs of Praise* and *Points of View* in 1961; *Animal Magic* in 1962; *The Sky at Night* in 1963; *Horizon* and *Match of The Day* in 1964; *World of Sport* 1965; *News at Ten* from 1967; *Gardeners' World* 1968; *Nationwide, Pot Black* and *Star Trek* (a US import, of course) in 1969.

. . . AND EIGHT LOST SHOWS

Less familiar names perhaps?

Harpers West One 1961–3, a department store drama featuring Wendy Richard.

Stars and Garters (1963–6) which harked back to the days of music hall and provided free cigarettes for the 'audience', but no alcohol.

United (1965–7), the adventures of a struggling football club.

Weavers Green (1966) featuring – briefly – two vets twice weekly.

Adam Adamant Lives! (1966–7) with actor Gerald Harper in false eyebrows.

Rainbow City (1967) the first drama series to lead with a black actor, Errol John.

Randall and Hopkirk (Deceased) (1969) featuring a ghostly detective.

Johnny Speight's *Curry and Chips* (also 1969) was pulled off air after only six episodes because of accusations of racial discrimination, together with excessive expletives from blacked-up Spike Milligan and a cast which included Kenny Lynch and Eric Sykes.

NOT FORGETTING THE CHILDREN'S PROGRAMMES

Although *Watch with Mother* had started in the 1950s, with a brief fifteen-minute daytime slot, the programme and many regular characters lingered through the 1960s and beyond – including *Bill and Ben* (who could have used a speech therapist), *The Woodentops*, *Andy Pandy* and *Rag, Tag and Bobtail.*

Blue Peter's first pet – in 1962 – was Petra the mongrel puppy who arrived wrapped up in Christmas paper but died of distemper two days later. She was hastily replaced from a pet shop in South London, with viewers unaware of the switch! The programme has the distinction of being the longest-running children's television programme in the world, having started its run in 1958. It has also been a prime fund-raiser for such diverse causes as Guide Dogs for the Blind (two purchased with 7½ tons of silver paper in 1964) and the RNLI (four lifeboats purchased with 240,000 paperbacks in 1967).

Playschool was the unplanned first programme for BBC2 in 1964 because of the 24-hour delay in the opening of the station.

Thunderbirds launched in 1965, with the 'lead' Scott Tracy said to be based on Sean Connery. It lasted for nearly a year. Puppet shows generally did well in the '60s: there was *Pinky and Perky* (1957–72);

Four Feather Falls in 1960 with the voices of Kenneth Connor and Nicholas Parsons; *Stingray* in 1964–5 featuring the first mute puppet Marina the Mermaid; *Captain Scarlet* (1967–8) with the captain's appearance allegedly based on Cary Grant, and *Joe 90* in 1968–9. *The Magic Roundabout* started out in 1965 and ran for eleven years, surviving an attempt at closure in 1968, when the fiercest petition for its return came from an army camp. *Sesame Street* and the *Clangers* arrived at the end of the decade. Interestingly, the more primitive puppets (i.e. glove puppets) such as *Sooty* (from the mid-'50s) and *Basil Brush* (from 1968 after a stint on David Nixon's television show) survived for much longer with *Sooty* setting a record for the longest surviving puppet show in its various guises.

The BBC took children's programming seriously – they disliked the idea of introducing 'sex' into children's television when puppeteer Harry Corbett proposed a panda girlfriend for Sooty in 1964. After some lengthy negotiations, it allowed Soo to join the show on condition she and Sooty did not touch! Two years later, they postponed an episode of *Pinky and Perky* because it was called 'You Too Can Be A P.M.' at the time of a forthcoming general election. When this episode was finally shown, it clashed with a political party broadcast from Harold Wilson – guess which programme had most viewers?

LAST, BUT NOT LEAST, THE ADVERTS

In 1960, the maximum time for commercials was reduced to 7½ minutes with only two breaks per hour. From August 1965, all cigarette commercials were banned from television and ITV lost £8,000,000 as a result. Their financial coffers were boosted by the mid-1960s with the introduction of celebrity endorsements – pioneered by Lux soap. Sandie Shaw, Ursula Andress and Diana Rigg were among the stars promoting this 'luxury' soap on screen. Joanna Lumley has attributed her acting career to the advertisement she did for Nimble bread at the end of 1969 – clad in a bikini and dangling in a balloon.

HALF A DOZEN SIXTIES SLOGANS

Cyril Lord (carpets): 'luxury you can afford'
Brylcreem: 'a little dab'll do ya'
'A Double Diamond Works Wonders'
'Beanz Meanz Heinz'
John Collier (menswear): 'the Window to Watch'
'Tick-a-tick-a Timex'

One ad that ran through the 1960s resulted in Mary Holland changing her name to Katie – her name in the Oxo ad. Well, everyone was already calling her Katie, so why not?

AND A FEW ADVERTISING FIRSTS

The first appearance of the Dulux Old English Sheepdog was in 1961, and the first, Shepton Dash, was the only one that was not a breed champion.

The first time that top ten pop stars featured in commercials was in 1963 when The Beatles sang about Jellimallo and the Rolling Stones about Rice Krispies.

The first colour ad was for Bird's Eye peas in November 1969.

HOMAGE TO RADIO

The BBC blamed television for declining interest in *Children's Hour* in 1961, and dropped the show after forty years. *Top of the Form*, a quiz show for secondary school pupils, moved from radio to television in 1962 again reflecting the demise of radio programmes. The 'Light Programme' as it was known ended in September 1967, and was replaced by music stations Radio 1 and Radio 2. (The 'Third Programme' and the 'Home Service' were also replaced – by Radio 3 and Radio 4.) One radio sitcom did survive: *The Navy Lark*. It ran from 1959 on the 'Light Programme' and survived on Radio 2 from 1962 until

1977, making it the longest-running sitcom on radio, and making stars of Jon Pertwee and Leslie Phillips (although Ronnie Barker was also lurking).

Round the Horne was transmitted weekly by the BBC from 1965 until 1969, following the successful format of *Beyond Our Ken* (1958–64) with camp comedy, *double entendres* and sexual innuendo. It is no surprise, then, to find Kenneth Williams featured prominently, voicing, among others, the world's dirtiest dirty old man, J. Peasemold Gruntfuttock. No one – from Noel Coward to the royal family – was safe from the programme's irreverent parodies until Kenneth Horne died, in 1969. Barry Took and Marty Feldman were the principal scriptwriters, succeeding in an arena many thought had died.

Britain's first radio soap was *Mrs Dale's Diary* which held on to listeners from 1948 to 1969, its final two years on Radio 2 (after being renamed *The Dales* in 1962). The Queen Mother was reputed to be a fan and has been said to comment that this was the only way 'one' could find out about what happened 'in a middle class family'!

But breaking all records – and still going strong on Radio 4 – is *The Archers*, which started life in 1951, and is now the world's longest-running soap opera. The actor Norman Painting, who played Phil Archer, holds the record for the longest-serving actor in a soap opera, as he played the role from 1951 until his death in 2009.

6

Science & Technology

THE AGE OF SPACE TRAVEL

When an American rocket went off course and crashed in Cuba in November 1960, killing a cow, the animal was given an official funeral as a victim of imperialist assassination – at least as far as Fidel Castro was concerned.

In January 1961, there was much happier news. A chimpanzee called Ham, named after the Holloman Aerospace Medical Centre, had survived a space flight, the nearest thing to a human success bearing in mind that the Russians had been using dogs for their test flights. Ham had been trained to pull levers (for banana pellet rewards) during his 5,000mph flight from Cape Canaveral which took him up 155 miles, beyond the stratosphere. Although the flight only lasted sixteen minutes, poor Ham had to wait three hours to be 'found' because his capsule had overshot its landing site in the Atlantic – but he finally got his reward, an apple and half an orange.

It is Russian Yuri Gagarin whose name lives on as the first man in space. His flight in Vostok 1 lasted 108 minutes in April 1961. Overnight he became a superstar, and received a film star welcome in London in July in an open silver Rolls-Royce with the registration YG1, upsetting glamorous songstress Yana (Guard) who had 'bought' this number (for £5!). America was only a month behind, with Alan Shepard, his flight lasting just 15 minutes in the tiny Freedom 7. But at least he actually arrived back inside Freedom 7, whereas Gagarin had been forced to land by parachute. Gagarin made news again in March 1968: he died when the training jet he was piloting crashed. Unexpectedly, the second, and the youngest, man in space – 25-year-old Gherman Titov in Russia's Vostok 2, August 1961 – suffered from motion sickness. Although this did not look good for his chosen career path, he actually seems to have spent more time in space, subsequently, than anyone else.

When Mariner 1 was launched from Cape Canaveral in July 1962 (towards Venus), it plunged into the Atlantic just four minutes after take-off. The plan had been that it would take 100 days to reach Venus and would then circle the planet and scan the enveloping cloud – but, thanks to human error, someone had omitted a very important minus sign from its computer-led instructions. A costly mistake – to the tune of over £4,000,000. Whoops.

Britain's Blue Streak was originally planned as a ballistic missile but spiralling costs, and other issues (e.g. the competition, the launching difficulties) meant that it was redeveloped as a part of the short-lived British space programme. It was launched as the first stage of a satellite launcher from Woomera in June 1964, and the successful launch was recorded for posterity by Pathé News. However, it was reliant on French and German components, which proved . . . unreliable. As a result, the Blue Streak became (a tad unfairly) known as the Civil Servant, i.e. 'it won't work and you can't fire it.'

The re-entry of Apollo 10 in May 1969 – which went within 9 miles of the moon's surface, the last American practice run before the trip to the moon – produced speeds of between 25,000 and 28,000mph, the fastest any human has travelled.

Although the historic moon landing in July 1969 was watched on television by millions around the world, it is unlikely that viewers took much notice of the space-suits. However, these were designed with twenty-one layers by Playtex, better known for their girdles and bras. Of the three astronauts on Apollo 11, only Neil Armstrong and Edwin 'Buzz' Aldrin set foot on the moon, in that order. Michael Collins remained in the command module while the others spent a couple of hours carrying out a number of exercises, planting the US flag and a plaque to go with it: 'We came in peace for all mankind'. Shame that the flag was then knocked over on their departure thanks to the blast, and the resultant flying dust and debris. Armstrong is also said to have left behind a small swatch of Clan Armstrong tartan to commemorate his first, and last, trip to the moon, and as a tribute to his forefathers! But the trio did not come back empty-handed, arriving with 45lb of rock samples. One of the minerals they discovered was named in their honour – armalcolite, i.e. **Arm**strong, **Al**drin, **Col**lins.

MORE SPACE FIRSTS

The first woman in space was Valentina Tereshkova (Russia) in June 1963. She circled the earth at the same time as Valery Bykovsky, who had already been in orbit for a couple of days, and they managed an electronic link-up which you could call the first space date.

The first spacewalk was by Russian Alexei Leonov in March 1965, lasting 12 minutes and 9 seconds at the end of a nylon cord for 3,000 miles.

The first landing (i.e. a soft, survivable, landing) on the moon was the unmanned Soviet Luna IX in February 1966. This resulted a few hours later in the first images to be sent from the moon itself.

The first spacecraft to land on another planet was the Venera III (Russian) which crash-landed on Venus in March 1966.

NASA's first successful manned mission was Apollo 7 in 1968 – and this was the site of the first live telecast from astronauts on board a manned US spacecraft, on 14 October.

It wasn't only dogs (in the 1950s) and chimps that were sent into space – the first tortoise in space was a Horsfield's tortoise that circumnavigated the moon in September 1968, making it the fastest tortoise in history.

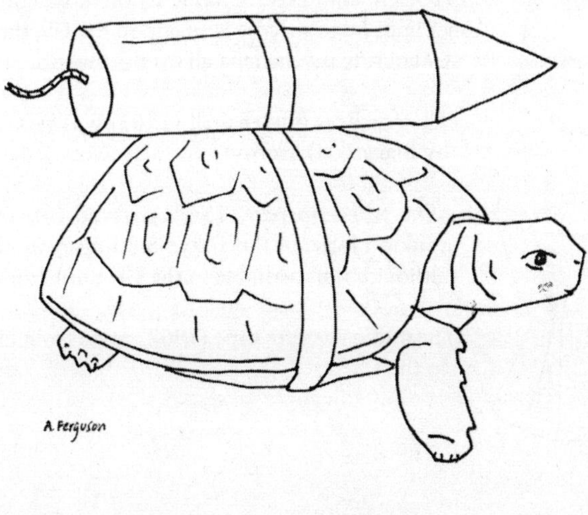

And not forgetting Britain. Ariel 3, the first satellite entirely designed in Britain, was launched into orbit to conduct experiments in May 1967, measuring noise, temperature, radiation and oxygen. It had been built at the space department of the Royal Aircraft Establishment in Farnborough, with the British Aircraft Corporation as the main contractor and the GEC supplying the electronics. (Although, yes, it was launched in the USA – but it did report its findings back to Slough!)

FLOATING SCIENCE

Sakura Maru, the first purpose-built floating trade fair, docked at Tilbury in June 1964 with 22,000 samples of Japanese goods on board. Gadgets included a transistor radio the size of a 2p piece, a tiny portable television which could plug into a car lighter socket, a public video-phone, plus the latest Japanese cars, motorbikes and bicycles. All demonstrated by geisha girls.

TEN GROOVY INVENTIONS

For drinkers of British pints, the no-nic (from 'no nick') glass arrived in 1960, with a strengthened bulge an inch from the rim, making it easier to stack.

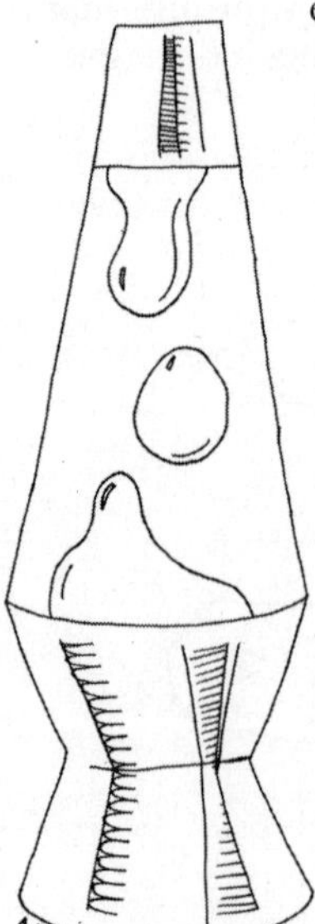

The astro lamp was the brainchild of Edward Craven Walker in Dorset, inspired by an unusual egg timer on a pub counter, and he introduced his design in 1963. He changed its name to the lava lamp and met with huge success here and in the US, the lamp symbolising psychedelia all over the world.

The cordless power drill (1961) was introduced by Black & Decker.

The fibre-tip pen (1962) arrived courtesy of Yukio Horie, of the Tokyo Stationery Company, although not available in the UK until 1967.

The audio cassette tape (1962) came from Philips, in the USA.

Silicone gel implants were invented in 1963 for breast augmentation to replace the use of silicone injections – by a plastic surgeon in Texas.

The computer mouse (between 1963–5) again in the US, was thought up by Douglas Endelbart. It was originally called an XY Position Indicator for a Display System!

The first Trimphone telephone was introduced by the GPO in 1965 and presented to a newly married couple by the Postmaster General. At least no one else gave them one.

The first automated teller machine or ATM was installed at a London branch of Barclay's Bank in 1967, invented (in the bath, apparently!) by John Shepherd-Barron from Scotland.

The jacuzzi (1968) arrived in the USA courtesy of Roy . . . Jacuzzi, who else?

LESS USEFUL INVENTIONS

An idea for walking on water came from a Mr M.W. Hulton. He demonstrated his sea-shoes on the Grand Union Canal in 1961 – they looked like two chunky skis cobbled together. Without a means of propulsion, or a following wind, the idea was, er, washed up.

In 1963, John Rinfret from Lincolnshire came up with an anti-theft bag. If someone tugged the bag, the owner pulled a concealed chain, emptying the contents of the bag on the pavement. So that meant your wallet could be picked up by anyone, and anything else in the bag would end up in the gutter. Nice one. Though, to be fair, he came up with much better ideas in subsequent years, winning the Queen's Award for Enterprise.

Japan, surely the mother of invention, came up with artificial breasts embedded with a heartbeat (1963) – to settle sleepless babies, of course, what else?

As for America, it's difficult to choose between Goodyear's illuminated tyres in 1961, or Thomas Bayard's vibrating toilet seat in 1966 (the latter to relieve constipation).

THE POWER GAME

Electricity was not as widespread in the 1960s as one might assume . . . the national target of 85 per cent electrification of the UK (including rural areas) was achieved as late as October 1964. Although both Bradwell (Essex) and Berkeley (Gloucestershire) Power Stations were built in the 1950s, they did not start generating electricity until 1962. By 1969, however, the age of electricity (and the labour-saving devices it spawned) had definitely arrived and two-thirds of households had a washing machine and a refrigerator. At the start of the 1960s, televisions boasted only two channels – in black and white – but by 1969, over 200,000 households in the country had colour sets.

The world's first tidal power station (and the only one in Europe) was opened in France, near St Mâlo on the Rance Estuary, by Charles de Gaulle in November 1966. Its operation had been held up for nearly a year by strikes and industrial action. Another source of power, this time British, was the first gas from the North Sea which was piped ashore in County Durham by BP in 1967. The first rig, Sea Gem, had started drilling in 1965 but collapsed the day after Boxing Day, killing thirteen. In 1969, the first British oil in the North Sea was discovered by non-British Amoco at Montrose, off Aberdeen, with Phillips Petroleum (more Americans) on its heels 80 miles off Humberside with what was then the richest strike to date.

As for nuclear power – on 21 October 1960, Her Majesty the Queen launched Britain's first nuclear submarine, HMS *Dreadnought*, at Barrow-in-Furness. (It became the first to surface through the ice of the North Pole – the Cold War, in every sense.) Three years later, Britain, Russia and the USA got together in sunny Moscow and signed a 'limited' nuclear test ban treaty. Britain's first Polaris-armed, ballistic nuclear submarine (following the perceived failure of Blue Streak), HMS *Resolution*, was officially launched by the Queen Mother in September 1966. This was the 1968 seat of the first Polaris missile to be successfully tested in the Atlantic by the Royal Navy, well behind the Americans, but becoming a useful deterrent patrol.

A very different kind of power was (and still is) the area of international communication. When the first artificial communications satellite, Telstar, started operating in July 1962, the world seemed a much smaller place because it carried television and telephone signals instantly across the Atlantic. The first television pictures from the USA made front-page news, in spite of the fact that the first transmission lasted just 60 seconds. However, Telstar had its own communication problems after just six months – probably due to the effects of radiation – and was replaced in 1963 by Telstar 2.

TOYS INVENTED IN THE SWINGING SIXTIES

Etch-A-Sketch arrived in 1960 courtesy of the Ohio Art Co. – and sold 50 million units in the next 25 years although it took a few years to take off in the UK. Lego had also just arrived in Britain from Denmark and sold, well, bucketloads, which was just as well as the warehouse containing their wooden toys burnt down in 1960, meaning they were pretty much reliant on the building blocks taking off. The name derives from 'leg godt' which means 'play well' in Danish.

1961 was the year of Scalextric – it was promoted by motor racing champion Jim Clark who acted as timekeeper in the first Scalextric World Championships in London in 1964. For girls, 1963 saw the arrival of the Sindy doll in her inaugural 'weekender' outfit, as a British rival to Barbie. Sindy's boyfriend Paul (allegedly named after Macca) arrived in 1965 and her little sister (Patch) in 1966, but the latter was made in Hong Kong.

For the young set, Mr Potato Head – the plastic version – was in the shops in 1964. No more borrowing a real potato from mum.

Spirograph launched in 1965, and was Toy of the Year by 1967. The swirly or geometric patterns it produced were perfectly in tune with the psychedelic and Pop Art trends around.

By 1966, the effects of the big (and small) screen were clear with the arrival of Action Man, supposedly based on TV's *Danger Man*, and the James Bond Aston Martin from Corgi.

Tiny Tears, the doll who wet her nappy, arrived from the USA (where else) in 1966, the same year that Twister was released, a good way to make (close) friends.

In 1967, children could play with KerPlunk (the falling marble game) or Battleships (naval warfare), and the Frisbee arrived. A year later, the media's influence came back into play: with the choice of a plastic yellow submarine from Corgi (inspired by guess who?) or the Batman utility belt (which had been launched in the US two years earlier) minus its bat-shark repellent and anti-Penguin pill.

The decade ended on more of a low, with Silly String (which was actually nothing like string) and Hot Wheels both of which were hits in 1969, Hot Wheels managing Toy of the Year thanks to its speed, or perhaps the lack of competition.

ELEVEN BRITISH NOBEL PRIZE WINNERS FROM THE WORLD OF SCIENCE

In 1960, Peter Medawar received the Medicine prize for his work on graft rejection and intolerance. He was born and lived briefly in Rio de Janeiro, his father a naturalised Brit.

In 1962, John Kendrew and Max Perutz received Chemistry prizes following their work with molecular structures.

Francis Crick and Maurice Wilkins achieved the accolade in 1962 for Physiology or Medicine as a result of their work with DNA. Wilkins was born in New Zealand but to Irish parents and came to the UK at the age of six.

Alan Hodgkin and Andrew Huxley were 1963 recipients (Physiology or Medicine) for nerve cell membrane work.

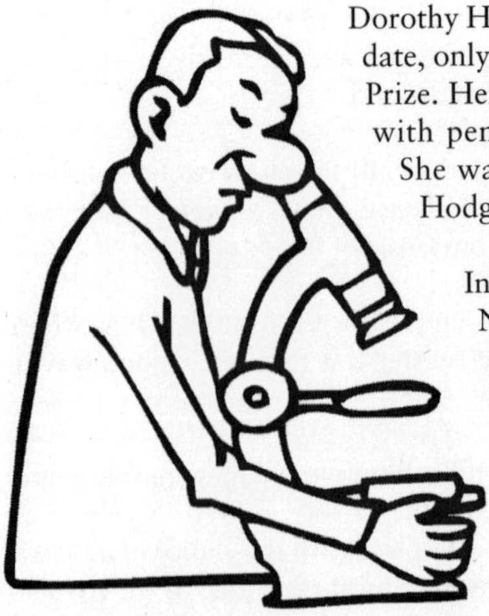

Dorothy Hodgkin became the first (and, to date, only) British woman to win a Nobel Prize. Her Chemistry prize for her work with penicillin was awarded in 1964. She was related by marriage to Alan Hodgkin – an impressive family!

In 1967, it was the turn of Ronald Norrish and George Porter – their Chemistry prize followed their work on fast chemical reactions.

Finally, in 1969, the concept of conformation (the behaviour of organic molecules) was the specialism of Derek Barton (Chemistry).

Incidentally, the Bank of Sweden inaugurated a new Nobel Prize in 1969 – for economic sciences; in memory of, naturally, Alfred Nobel.

THE AGE OF THE TRANSPLANT

Dr Christian Barnard carried out the first successful heart transplant at Cape Town in December 1967, giving a 55-year-old grocer a few more weeks of life. Britain's first heart transplant a year later took place at the National Heart Hospital in Marylebone, London. The patient was named Fred West – but not that Fred West. It was lucky for all of us that Dr Barnard did not put aside his career to concentrate on his daughter's attempt to become a world champion water skier as was once planned. Deirdre became a champion, anyway.

Less famously, it is on record that the same Dr Barnard completed a successful head transplant in 1960, also in Cape Town – on a dog. Russia and the USA had already tried head transplants on dogs.

In Britain, the first kidney transplant (using a living donor) took place with 49-year-old twin brothers at the Edinburgh Royal in 1960. The first lung transplant also took place here, in May 1968, after 15-year-old Alex Smith mistook weed killer for lemonade (he survived twelve days). Similarly, Addenbrooke's in Cambridge started their pioneering transplant programme in the 1960s.

1969 saw the first human eye transplant – in Houston, Texas – hailed as a miracle, though it failed to restore patient John Madden's sight.

AND THE AGE OF THE 'PLANNED' FAMILY

The first contraceptive pill went on sale in the UK in January 1961, although it was not then available on the NHS. This liberating event happened in June 1963. Between 1962 and 1969, the NHS website shows that the number of women taking the pill rose from 50,000 to 1,000,000.

Philip Larkin wrote ('Annus Mirabilis' in the '70s) that sexual intercourse began in 1963, too late for him, but not too late for Helen

Brook who opened her first Advisory Centre in London in July 1964. Advice on birth control for young (under-25) unmarried women was not popular with every sector of society, however. Moral campaigners Mary Whitehouse and Lord Longford were at this time waiting in the wings. Birmingham was the next port of call for Brook in 1966, and many more urban locations in the UK followed.

David Steel was the man behind the 1967 Abortion Act and legal abortions from 1968 are largely thanks to him. The first abortion clinic opened in October 1968 (in the capital, not unexpectedly).

Epidural pain relief during childbirth was used for the first time in 1968, providing a little bit of encouragement for those who actually did want to give birth. This may have encouraged Essex girl Irene Hanson to produce Britain's first live quintuplets of the twentieth century. Her five baby girls were born in November 1969, having been detected in the womb by a new British invention, the ultrasound detector.

For those who wanted to give birth but had little hope, Cambridge University removed human eggs from volunteers to be fertilised in a test tube, bringing hope from 1969 for such families.

Or, for those opting for 'the snip', the first vasectomy clinic opened in Cardiff in 1968. Birmingham followed in 1969 with a charge of £16 per head, well, not head, but rather lower.

MEDICAL MARVELS

The first hearing aids issued by the NHS arrived in June 1960, and the first 'soft' contact lenses became popular in the 1960s.

Pregnant women were still being prescribed thalidomide at the beginning of the 1960s to treat morning sickness or insomnia, but it was withdrawn from sale in 1961 after babies were born with limb deformities and other disabilities.

In March 1963, valium was introduced by Swiss company Hoffman-La Roche (the world's largest drug company), amid claims that it was a new wonder drug. However, these claims were based on the calming effect the drug had on circus lions and tigers. Hmm.

Although prescription charges were free from 1 February 1965, there was an about turn in 1968 when they were reintroduced – at a higher rate of 2*s* 6*d*, an increase of 6*d*. Thanks to the Labour Government for this one.

The first patent issued by the US to a king was for a device to monitor the function of the human heart. In 1969, this was patented by King Hassan II of Morocco. Donating a few million pounds for heart research would probably have been even more useful.

DIFFERENT SCIENCES

Anthropology? Natural Science? These have not been forgotten, just cut to a few bare bones . . . literally.

Jacques Cousteau published his new deep ocean discoveries in November 1968. One such discovery was that captive squids suffering from depression commit suicide by eating their own tentacles. Fascinating stuff. He is better known, however, for his work in ocean ecology and experimenting with underwater habitats for humans. Half a dozen men managed to live for thirty days 10 metres under the Red Sea in 1963 in an underwater village called Conshelf II, spawning a new word – oceanauts.

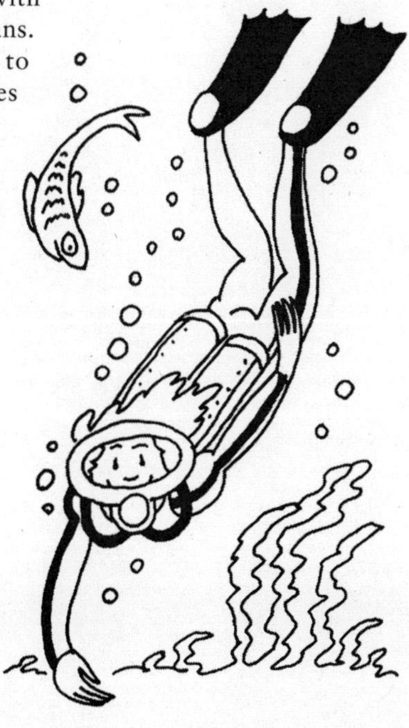

In Kenya in 1961, British anthropologists Louis and Mary Leakey uncovered some of the bones of a child (including the skull) regarded as the missing link between ape and man and dating back 14,000,000 years. A few years later, in Tanzania, the team found bones, which, although not nearly so old (only 1.75 million years!), were accompanied by stone tools and thus designated the earliest tool-maker, Homo Habilis, or Handy Andy.

A three hundred-year-old skull was dug up in the grounds of 10 Downing Street in March 1962. Harold Macmillan was a bit busy being Prime Minister to pursue the matter further.

The oldest tortoise in the world, Tui Malila, died in 1965, aged 188. She had been given to the King of Tonga in 1777 by Captain Cook – it's safe to say the king hadn't realised what a lengthy commitment he'd made.

7

Travel & Transport

By 1960, 28 per cent of British households had a car, and that was 45 per cent by 1969. In 1965, there were thirteen million cars on British roads, double that of 1955. To cash in, traffic wardens appeared, hitting London with 344 parking tickets on their first day in September 1960. The very first ticket (for £2) was waived after a public outcry – because the car belonged to a doctor attending a patient in Westminster having a heart attack! Other controls arrived:

MOT testing introduced for cars over ten years old in 1960.

First push-button Panda crossings were in use from April 1962.

A 50mph limit on all trunk roads was imposed in 1963.

Continental road traffic signs were introduced in 1963.

The first pedestrian schemes were developed in 1963 in London.

Box junctions with yellow cross-hatchings introduced, also in London, 1964.

The 70mph speed limit on motorways started in 1965, enforceable from 1967, leading to 20 per cent reduction in casualties.

Seatbelts became compulsory in new cars from 1967.

By 1967, MOT testing was required on cars over three years old.

The first speeding British motorist breathalysed was in Somerset in October 1967. Road deaths fell by over 22 per cent in the winter following its introduction.

Pelican crossings were introduced in 1969.

CARS AND MORE CARS

In 1961, the millionth Morris Minor came off the British assembly line with the Mini following suit in 1965. New models in the 1960s included:

E-type Jag 1961 (hard-top coupé £2,196 or open-top £2,097 – half the price of a house).

Renault 4 Hatchback (the first family hatchback) and the Mini Cooper in 1961.

Ford Cortina (around £500) and Triumph Spitfire in 1962.

The world's smallest car, the Peel P50 (a three-wheel, one-door microcar produced on the Isle of Man), weighing 132lb and measuring 54in long x 20in wide, 1962.

Vauxhall Viva and Hillman Imp, 1963.

Aston Martin DB6 (their first four seater), 1965. This was also the year of the first Panda car.

Hillman Hunter (Scotland) and Toyota Corolla (Japan), 1966.

Jaguar XJ6 (saloon) and Ford Escort, 1968. (Although actor Harrison Ford, a male escort in the 1960s, could qualify as the first Ford Escort!)

Austin Maxi and Ford Capri, 1969.

While the M1 started life in 1959, the M2 didn't open until 1963, bypassing the Medway towns, the only motorway which doesn't connect to another. Although not the first motorway services, Forton Services (on the M6 near Lancaster from 1965) and Leicester Forest East on the M1 became memorable in the 1960s for different reasons.

Forton housed the Tower Restaurant with views over Morecambe Bay, a hexagon resembling an aircraft control tower. For an even better dining experience, the Captain's Table (furnished by Terence Conran) at Leicester Forest East entered the *Good Food Guide* in 1968. Scratchwood Services (now London Gateway) opened in 1969 in the firing line for the guns of HMS *Belfast*, the museum ship moored beside Tower Bridge, 12½ miles away, serving as a reminder of the power of naval gunnery (and perhaps the disposability of motorway services). Blue Boar Services – now Watford Gap – which opened at the same time as the M1, was so seemingly popular with the rock 'n' roll fraternity that Jimi Hendrix apparently thought it was a club, so often was the name Blue Boar mentioned by his peers.

There were a number of famous celebrity links to particular cars in the 1960s. John Lennon's Rolls-Royce Phantom V arrived as a matt-black model in 1965, but by 1967 John had commissioned a psychedelic design based on that of a gypsy wagon in his garden. A spokesman for Rolls-Royce regarded the change as 'unfortunate' and at least one passer-by shouted abuse at such a desecration of an English icon!

Another Rolls-Royce owner, Fanny Cradock, the television chef, was charged with careless driving in 1964 after she refused to move her Rolls which was holding up the traffic while she chatted to a friend. She called the policeman who cautioned her 'a uniformed delinquent' and reversed into the car behind because 'he told me to back up. I was just doing what I was told!' Owners of the Mini at this time, often adorned in patriotic red/white/blue, included Twiggy, Brigitte Bardot, The Beatles and Lord Snowdon, icons of a different kind, but reinforcing the popularity – and sales – of the car. The prominence

of some cars on screen also had a tremendous impact on sales: for instance, the Mini Cooper that famously featured in *The Italian Job* (sometimes known as the Giant Killer because of its success in the Monte Carlo Rally in 1964, 1965 and 1967 – a souped-up version, that is), the Lotus Elan driven by Diana Rigg in *The Avengers*, and James Bond's Aston Martin DB5 in *Goldfinger.*

London saw several 'firsts' for motorists. The first British mini cabs started in Wimbledon in March 1961 as Carline, and the first British self-service petrol station opened on Southwark Bridge in 1962. The same year, the first large-scale underpass in London was opened at Hyde Park, its 1961 construction the subject of a painting by Bernard Dunstan, who usually painted nudes . . . this was also the location for what was then the largest underground car park (also opened in 1962, for as many as 1,000 cars).

Not forgetting the ladies behind the wheel: 16-year-old Mandy Rice-Davies, involved in the Profumo scandal, arrived in London as the rather more innocent 'Miss Austin' at the 1960 Earls Court Motor Show. As for Barbara Castle, the Minister of Transport between 1965 and 1968, she didn't have a driving licence at the time she introduced the 70mph speed limit and the breathalyser. Remaining in London, the city's first female cabbie from April 1967 was Mrs Shirley Preston.

And some tales of the unexpected . . . in 1968, the Duke of Bedford was fined £50 for undertaking on the M1, and was very easy to find as his number plate was DOB1. Just as unlucky were the organisers of the ROSPA exhibition at Harrogate that year – because their entire display fell down, though serious injury was avoided!

ON TWO WHEELS

At the beginning of the decade, most families had at least one bike, especially in rural areas. Even schoolchildren had a bike, and they were used by a large majority of factory workers. Raleigh, one of the oldest bicycle companies in the world, took advantage of the popularity of the bike at this time, producing the folding bike in 1965 and the Chopper (originally for children) in 1969. They were not the first to produce the small-wheeled bicycle, though, losing out to the Moulton Bicycle Company who launched their version at Earls Court in 1962: a mini-bike to go with mini-skirts and Mini cars.

Speeding things up a notch, it was the 1960s Mod who popularised the scooter – Lambrettas and Vespas, to be precise – to be even more precise, the Lambretta GT200 and the Vespa GS160. Rockers were still riding the Triumph and Norton motorbikes beloved of the 1950s Teddy Boys. Interesting that the Mods went for Italian style (adding lights, mascots, crash bars and the rest) while the Rockers stuck with British utility.

FLYING HIGH

Record-breakers of the decade included:

The RAF's English Electric Lightning was the first British operational aircraft capable of achieving twice the speed of sound, i.e. over 1,200mph, from 1960. The first civil airliner to break the sound barrier at 662.5mph was a Canadian Pacific DC-8 in August 1961, when it also achieved an altitude record of 50,000ft.

TWA became the first airline to show in-flight films on a regular basis in 1961.

The first plane to go faster than 4,000mph was the X-15 in November 1961, achieving 4,070mph for 86 seconds over California. It is rumoured that the pilot, Robert White, was booked for speeding on his way home.

Geraldine Monk (from West Germany) became the first woman to complete a solo flight around the world – in April 1964.

The world's fastest jet plane that made its first flight in December 1964 was the Lockheed SR-71 Blackbird.

The first automatic aeroplane landing was achieved by a BEA Trident flying Paris to Heathrow in June 1965.

The Hawker-Siddeley Harrier, the world's first aircraft with vertical take-off and landing, was unveiled at the Farnborough Air Show in September 1968.

The Boeing 747 was the world's largest aeroplane at the time of its maiden flight in February 1969, as long as a football field and as tall as a six-storey house – and constructed in the world's largest building in Washington. Its size brought out the sceptics who felt catastrophe would soon follow.

The Concorde 001 became the first passenger aircraft to break the sound barrier, in October 1969, after an earlier successful maiden flight. The official unveiling at Toulouse, in 1967, had been memorable for the French version of the British national anthem – ooh la-la.

Gatwick was the first airport in the world to combine a trunk road facility, an air terminal and rail travel, at the beginning of the 1960s. The terminal and runways were both enlarged during this period. This was where Freddie Laker launched his budget Laker Airways (later Skytrain) in 1966, starting with a couple of second- hand BOAC planes, offering flights to or from New York for just $100. Even busier was (and is) Heathrow (London Airport before it was renamed in 1966) – with around 5.5 million passengers in 1960, the figure trebled by the end of the '60s. It, too, added to its terminals and runways extensively – although they both seem to have underestimated the amount of car parking needed . . . there had been an assumption that flying was pretty much for the rich and such passengers would arrive with chauffeurs! To some extent, this problem was alleviated with the opening of BEA's West London Air Terminal (from the late 1950s/ early '60s) where passengers could check in before being bussed to Heathrow. Another terminal erected over two of the platforms at London's Victoria station (opened May 1962) would serve for some

of the other burgeoning airlines. Travellers in those early heady days tended to be suited and booted, could check in just 15 minutes before their flight and smoke on board. As for air stewardesses, they wore regulation nail varnish, pill-box hats and white gloves, even serving soup for first class passengers from a tureen . . . those were the days.

Daredevils appeared in the air, too. The Red Arrows – the RAF acrobatic team – was formed in 1964, first with five planes, ending up with nine by 1968. The team introduced themselves to the media with a display in Gloucestershire in March 1965, but their first public display a few months later was, less patriotically, in France. One of the team's founders was to give a personal demonstration in April 1968, flying his Hawker Hunter jet fighter underneath the top span of Tower Bridge. This was 32-year-old flight Flight Lieutenant Alan Pollock who was protesting at the lack of a flypast to celebrate the RAF's 50th anniversary. As a result, the RAF wanted him court martialled, the police wanted him tried in a civil court, but neither in fact ever happened.

CAN YOU ANSWER THESE?

Q1. What happened to The Beatles at the BOAC terminal at Victoria in June 1966 as they were about to embark on a world tour?
Answer: They were vaccinated against cholera.

Q2. What kind of trouble was Jimi Hendrix in (with customs) when he arrived at Heathrow in August 1967?
Answer: Nothing to do with drugs! He had a gas gun for 'personal protection', allowed in the States but illegal here.

Q3. Why were Spitfires used predominantly in the 1969 film *The Battle of Britain*, rather than Hurricanes which actually dominated the battle?
Answer: Because, at the time, there was a shortage of Hurricanes in flying condition for the air combat scenes. Group Captain Hamish Mahaddie had the job of tracking down the aircraft for the film, and did get hold of the last six Hurricanes in the world, three of which were not able to fly. He also bought 50 retired Messerschmidts, not from the Germans, but from the Spanish Air Force!

ON THE WATERS

By the 1960s, air travel had impacted on the demand for giant passenger liners, and the *Carthage* was an early casualty, being sold to Japan for scrap in March 1961 after thirty years' service. However, the *Oriana* and the *Canberra* were faster and larger and dominated the Australia service during the decade. Glasgow-built *QE2* was designed for a new cruising era and was launched in September 1967. Unfortunately, her maiden voyage, to New York from Southampton, did not take place until May 1969 because of technical problems, but she was greeted at Manhattan with a spectacular gala reception, the last of its kind. En route, there was a christening and a funeral (of a steward who was buried at sea). The *Queen Elizabeth* had been refitted for cruising in 1965 but this was soon seen as uneconomic and she set off for Florida in 1968 to become a hotel and tourist attraction for a couple of years before being sold. The *Queen Mary* was sold to the town of Long Beach in California in October 1967, and left Southampton on her final voyage with a London bus on board. It was the RMS *Carinthia* that had one of the most unfortunate experiences on arriving in New York – this was in December 1964, during the era of the McCarthy communist witch-hunts. The crew were all questioned, and on being

asked 'Are you a commy?' one agreed that he was. He thought he was being asked if he was a commis chef but Immigration Officers were not amused. This liner, too, was sold in 1968.

By 1960, the commercial traffic on Britain's canals had all but disappeared. Thousands of miles of canals were filled in around Glasgow and Manchester and thousands of miles still lay derelict, but things started to improve when the British Waterways Board was created in 1962. By then, the voluntary sector had already been involved in saving the canal heritage, Stratford-upon-Avon being a prime example, reopened by the Queen Mother in February 1964. In 1968, the Transport Act allowed further development for leisure and, in London, canal towpaths appeared for walkers and bikers. By now, the holiday boating industry had really taken off. Canals had become an asset rather than an industrial blight. At the end of the '60s, docklands areas also started shifting their emphasis from industry to leisure.

In June 1965, around fifty crofters protested at the first Sunday ferry crossing from the Scottish mainland to the Isle of Skye. They regarded the Sunday boat service as a 'desecration of the biblical Sabbath'. Presbyterian Reverend Angus Smith became known as the Ferry Reverend after he lay down on the slipway as part of the protest, and was forcibly removed by a bunch of burly policemen. The tourist industry the ferry opened up may have been some compensation for the crofters.

The first regular hovercraft passenger service started in 1962 when just twenty-four passengers – and 8,000 letters – were carried across the Dee from Rhyl to Wallasey. A summertime service was also started that year between Portsmouth and Ryde and an experimental service ran across the Bristol Channel in 1963. Rather more passengers were attracted to the Ramsgate to Calais service, whose first hovercraft skimmed across the Channel in April 1966 – even General de Gaulle used the service. The Hoverferry, launched in August 1968 with a journey time of 35 minutes from Dover to Boulogne, was the first able to carry cars, 30 of them, with 254 passengers. Less well known was the use of hovercraft in 1968 for a British army unit serving in the Far East, and for American servicemen in Vietnam – ideal over the swampy ground. In 1969, Hoverlloyd built a Hoverport at Pegwell Bay (near Ramsgate) and the Calais Hoverport opened – the heyday of hover had arrived.

SAD ENDINGS AND NEW BEGINNINGS – FOR TRAINS

The last steam locomotive was built for British Railways in March 1960, and the last steam train on London's Underground system was retired in 1961 after serving part of the Metropolitan line – although a non-passenger steam train did continue to carry waste (and night maintenance staff!) between Neasden and Watford every day for a number of years. Similarly, Britain's last regular steam passenger service, which ran between Brockenhurst and Lymington in Hampshire, finished puffing in April 1967. 'Farewell to Steam', indeed, and this was the name of the last trip on the old Liverpool to Carlisle route in August 1968. The 1960s is also associated with Dr Beeching, whose infamous 1963 report proposed axing nearly 5,000 miles of track, over 2,000 stations and around 70,000 jobs over seven years – all in an attempt to make British Rail more profitable (it had been losing £140 million a year!).

When the old Euston station in London was redeveloped in 1962, protests from such as John Betjeman could not save the historic façade. The new station rose from the ashes in 1968, and was opened by Her Majesty the Queen in October of that year. The gothic exterior of St Pancras, however, which was also faced with demolition in

1966, was saved. This time, Sir John Betjeman's intervention resulted in the building receiving a Grade I listing even though he had felt that the building might be 'too beautiful and too romantic to survive'.

More good news came in the form of the first Trans-Pennine diesel express trains introduced in January 1961 between Liverpool and Hull. Work on two new rail links to Heathrow started in 1968, one of them an extension to the Piccadilly underground line.

Similar events were happening overseas – sad news in that the last journey of the Orient Express Paris to Istanbul service was in May 1961, ending the era of luxury, known as the King of Trains and the Train of Kings (although other variants on other routes continued). But good news for Japan, whose Bullet Train started life in 1964, days before Japan's first Olympics. It was originally called the Shinkansen, meaning new trunk line or new main line, with the name 'Bullet' derived from its shape. It operated between Tokyo and Osaka, reducing the time to travel the 325 miles from over 6½ hours to just over 3 hours.

A TRIO OF RAIL FIRSTS . . .

February 1961 saw the first automatic half-barrier level crossing (at Spath, near Uttoxeter). It was described by the *Daily Mail* as the first 'robot crossing'.

The first train journey by a Pope for 99 years was in October 1962, on a 400-mile journey from Loreto to Assisi. Not difficult to work out which country this was.

1964 was the year that the Pleasure Beach at Blackpool purchased Britain's first monorail 'the transport of the future' – from the World's Fair in Lausanne, Switzerland. It didn't actually open until 1966, though, so technically Billy Butlin's monorail at Skegness in 1965 was the first, operationally speaking.

AND OVER TO THE UNDERGROUND . . .

In September 1960, the first travelator opened at Bank station on the London Underground. 1964 was the year of the first automatically controlled tube trains on the Central line; and the first automatic ticket barrier – at Stamford Brook. In 1968, the first section of the new Victoria line opened (the first fully automated line), the first to cross central London in sixty years. The line cost an eye-watering £75 million plus, and was officially 'blessed' in March of the following year by Her Majesty the Queen, the first reigning monarch to make a journey on the system. Hope she had a valid ticket.

A LOOK BACK AT BUSES AND TRAMS

On 8 October 1960, the last English city said goodbye to its tram network – Sheffield. They were sent for scrap after over eighty years' service, and even Brian Jones (the Rolling Stones guitarist) was said to have made a pilgrimage to 'see them off'. Some of these nostalgia-laden vehicles were, however, saved, ending up at the National Tramway Museum at Crich in Derbyshire. Even one of the horse trams dating from 1874 was put on display at Crich, from 1963, and the first electric trams ran there in 1964: the museum evolved as the Crich Tramway Village in 1967. Scotland lost its last trams, in Glasgow, in 1962, the last major city in Britain to succumb to the twentieth century. Note the return, though, of the Supertram to Sheffield and other areas at the turn of the twenty-first century! Blackpool is the

only place to hang on to a limited 'traditional' tram service, which celebrated its 75th anniversary in September 1960, and still serves the seafront as far as the suburb of Fleetwood. Seaton in Devon also went against the national trend when the closed BR line was purchased in 1969 to introduce a 3-mile tram connection between the seaside town and nearby Colyton.

Trolleybuses suffered a similar demise at this time. The last trolleybuses in London ran in May 1962, after over 100 had been sold to Spanish operators. However, routes in other cities continued until later in the '60s. In 1969, four groups of enthusiasts established a Trolleybus Museum at Sandtoft, near Doncaster, on a derelict Second World War airfield.

Although over 4,000 staff were recruited from the West Indies by London Transport between 1956 and 1970, there was, in 1963, still a shortage of bus drivers, so, at the request of the Maltese Government, representatives visited the island and engaged a number of road (and rail) operating staff. A long way to commute! The popular open-platform Routemaster buses that had run in London since the 1950s started to be phased out from 1967 when one-man buses were legalised (no more bus conductors or clippies). The last Routemaster – which had the same brakes as a Centurion tank! – was built in 1968 although they continued to run for many more years. The first Museum of British Transport was opened in 1961 in, appropriately, an old bus garage in Clapham, South London, ensuring that the Routemaster – and other buses, trams, and trains – would live on. It has since moved out of London although the London Transport Museum remains.

8

THIS SPORTING LIFE

THE BEAUTIFUL GAME

Denis Law scored six times for Manchester City against Luton in an FA Cup tie in 1961, but ended up on the losing side because the match was abandoned owing to heavy rain, and Luton won the rearranged fixture. Lucky was obviously not his middle name, because in 1968, when sitting in the dug-out having sustained an injury during the Manchester United v Real Madrid European Cup semi-final, he punched the air after a Manchester goal and sent his fist through the low ceiling, sustaining further injury.

In 1961, Barrow FC did not have floodlights, and Gillingham needed to arrive in good time for the 5.15 p.m. kick-off in their October match. They missed their train because of heavy traffic, had to charter a plane at a cost of £500 to pick them up from Heathrow (after negotiating a 5.30 p.m. kick-off on the telephone), and arrived at Blackpool, 70 miles away, in pouring rain 105 minutes before the allotted start time. This just gave them time for the fastest change of clothes in history – but not enough to recover from the fraught journey, as Gillingham lost 7–0, the score standing although the game was abandoned at 7.00 p.m. owing to failing light! Barrow was in the news again in 1968. This time, the referee received congratulatory pats on the back from the Barrow team at the end of their 1968 home game against Plymouth Argyle, having 'scored' the only goal of the match when he deflected the ball past the Plymouth goalkeeper.

If luck does play a part in football, then it certainly ran out for Bryn and Ray Jones (not related) playing for Chester FC on New Year's Day in 1966. Both full-backs broke a leg in the match against Aldershot. Chester's victory (3–2) may have been a minor compensation. It had to be a lot more than just bad luck, though, when all twenty-two players (plus one linesman!) were booked by the referee in a 'good, hard game' between Tongham and Hawley Youth Clubs in November 1969 (won by Tongham 2–0). The *Guinness Book of Records* describes this as the 'most undisciplined football match ever'.

While own goals by goalkeepers are not unheard of, the one by Gary Sprake, the Leeds United goalkeeper, at Anfield in 1967 has gone down in history because, during the half-time interval, the DJ chose to play Des O'Connor's 'Careless Hands'. The crowd reprised the song every time poor Gary returned to play against Liverpool.

Four months before England's momentous World Cup victory in July 1966 (a 4–2 victory over West Germany in case you are the one person who hadn't heard), the Jules Rimet trophy – the World Cup – disappeared from its showcase in Westminster Central Hall despite 24-hour security. It was recovered by Pickles the dog from a garden in South London, a dog proclaimed at the time as having succeeded where Scotland Yard had failed. The reward (accounts vary between £6,000 and £9,000) went to the dog's owner, not the dog, which seems a bit unfair. Sadly – and coincidentally – both Pickles and the then Chairman of the Football Association, Joe Mears, died within a year, with stress perhaps playing its part.

AND HERE ARE A DOZEN FOOTBALL FIRSTS

The first English football league match to be televised was played between Blackpool and Bolton Wanderers in September 1960.

Denis Law set what was then a record £55,000 transfer fee in 1960 when he moved from Huddersfield to Manchester City. He beat the record again when transferring from Manchester to Torino in 1961 for £100,000, and for a third time when transferring from Torino to Manchester United in 1962 for £115,000.

Danny Blanchflower, captain of Tottenham Hotspur, and a Northern Ireland international player, became the first celebrity to decline an invitation to have his story featured on *This is Your Life* (February 1961).

Johnny Haynes (England and Fulham) was the first footballer to receive £100 a week after the cap of £20 a week was abolished in 1961. (Who said bring back the cap?)

Bobby Moore made the first of his record 108 appearances for England's football squad when he played against Peru in the 1962 World Cup. Moore became the youngest ever England captain the following year against Czechoslovakia when he was 22 years and 47 days – England won 4–2.

In 1963, Tottenham Hotspur became the first British team to win the European Cup Winners' Cup. They beat Atlético Madrid 5–1 in Rotterdam in May.

The first recipient of the Football Sword of Honour for distinguished service to British and international football was Matt Busby, manager of Manchester United (December 1964).

Stanley Matthews, the 'Wizard of the Dribble', became the first British footballer to be knighted – in the 1965 New Year's Honours. A month later, he played his last match for Stoke, aged 50 years and 5 days, the oldest player to compete in a football league match.

It was Geoff Hurst who scored a hat-trick to secure England's victory in the World Cup in 1966 – the first such feat in a World Cup final.

The first ever all-London FA Cup final was won by Tottenham Hotspur against Chelsea, 2–1, in May 1967. This became known as the Cockney Cup Final (although neither Tottenham or Chelsea are within the sound of Bow Bells).

Celtic were the first British club to win the European Cup, with a 2–1 win over Inter Milan in Lisbon in 1967, and no doubt the only team to be able to claim that all eleven players were born within 30 minutes of their home ground.

Alan Mullery became the first England player to be sent off when he overreacted to a series of tackles in Florence against Yugoslavia in June 1968. Not a record he would have wanted.

And perhaps the first war following a football match was the one in June 1969 between El Salvador and Honduras – their three matches in rounds for the FIFA World Cup had resulted in a high level of violence, and one suicide (turned into a martyrdom). The border clashes evolved into military action, with El Salvador coming off worse – unlike in the football matches. A smaller country, but they stood up to the Hondurans both on and off the field until their troops withdrew in August.

WINNING ON THE WATER

Francis Chichester was arguably the Sailor of the Sixties. He was the first winner of the single-handed trans-Atlantic yacht race in 1960. The trip in *Gipsy Moth III* took him 40 days, knocking 16 days off the previous record, a record he broke again in 1964 with a crossing of just 30 days. His even bigger test came in 1966 when he set off in *Gipsy Moth IV* to sail around the world, starting from Plymouth. It took him one day over nine months, the first (with only one port of call – Sydney) and fastest circumnavigation by a small yacht and including the longest unbroken journey made by a small yacht – 15,517 miles from Australia to Plymouth via Cape Horn. All achieved by a cancer survivor who could have been sitting at home, enjoying his old age pension. When he was knighted (in July 1967) on the quay at Greenwich, Queen Elizabeth II apparently used the same sword that had been used to knight another sailing Francis – Sir Francis Drake. Almost as big an honour was seeing his face soon afterwards on a stamp, bearing in mind that he was neither royal nor dead.

Donald Campbell became the first man to break the world land and water speed records in the same year – 1964. In July, he broke the land speed record on the salt flats at Lake Eyre in Australia, travelling at 403.1mph. At the end of the year (New Year's Eve) he reached 276.33mph in his speedboat on Lake Dumbleyung in Perth after being delayed by bad weather and moulting ducks. Tragically, just a few years later (4 January 1967) he was killed on Coniston Water in the Lake District, on his second attempt to break his own record; at the time, divers found only his helmet and his teddy bear mascot, Mr Whoppit.

British greengrocer and part-time sailor Alec Rose had saved hard (really hard) to finance his round-the-world solo voyage – some 28,500 miles, with stops in Australia and New Zealand. He was at sea for just under a year, arriving home on 4 July 1968, and was knighted just days later.

The first east–west and west–east solo rowers across the Atlantic both completed their epic performances in 1969. British rower John Fairfax, who described himself as a professional adventurer, rowed from the Canaries to Florida, arriving in July 1969 after 180 days, making him the first solo rower of any ocean. Irishman Tom McClean, ex-SAS, did the reverse journey, from Newfoundland to Ireland, in 70 days, arriving eight days later than Fairfax (17 May to 27 July 1969). This latter record is remarkable when compared with British paratroopers Captain John Ridgway and Sergeant Chay Blyth who had rowed the Atlantic from Cape Cod to Ireland in 92 days three years earlier with twice the manpower.

Edward 'Ted' Heath (the Conservative Prime Minister from 1970–4) was the owner and skipper of *Morning Cloud*, the yacht that won the Sydney to Hobart sailing race in 1969. Quite an achievement for a man who had only begun sailing with lessons in a dinghy at Broadstairs in 1966! He became Captain of Britain's World Cup team while PM.

A BIT OF BOXING

Britain produced three world champions during the decade – Walter McGowan at flyweight, Howard Winstone at featherweight and Terry Downes at middleweight. Perhaps better known is the one who missed out (to Cassius Clay, the world heavyweight champion from 1964) – Henry Cooper, the British and Commonwealth heavyweight champion. Cooper won his first Lonsdale title in 1961, and, with his third in 1967, became the first to win three Lonsdale belts outright.

He also took the European heavyweight crown (in 1964, against Brian London) but didn't manage to beat Clay in 1963 or 1966, although he did put Clay on the floor in 1963. In the crowd at Wembley for the first of their fights were actors Liz Taylor and Richard Burton, who seemingly got spattered with blood from Henry's cut eye – the chance you take when you sit ringside. Luckier were actors Lee Marvin and George Raft, among the 45,000 at Arsenal's Highbury Stadium for the 1966 match. However, Cooper did manage to win the title of BBC Sports Personality of the Year in 1967, after a year without defeat, and was awarded the first OBE ever given to a boxer in 1969.

Prior to the success of Cassius Clay aka Muhammad Ali (stripped of his title when he refused conscription in 1967 'on religious grounds' after becoming a Muslim – the grounds rejected), also American, Rocky Marciano, had retired as the undefeated heavyweight world champion in the 1950s, but was to die in 1969 in an air crash. Another boxer who met a sudden and tragic end during this period was British former light heavyweight champion Freddie Mills who was found shot in the head in his car in July 1965 – suicide the more acceptable verdict than murder. This was the same man who had been knocked down by George the kangaroo when in a bout promoting the opening of the Christmas season of Bertram Mills' Circus in London in 1962. A far lesser tragedy was Scot Dick McTaggart's unexpected defeat in the light welterweight boxing final in the 1962 Commonwealth Games in Perth. However, his opponent, Ghanaian Clement Quartey, was so shocked to have beaten the favourite that he apparently fainted and was out cold for several minutes.

BEATLES & BOXING

Sonny Liston (American heavyweight champion of the world in 1962) had his Madame Tussaud's image on the cover of The Beatles' 1967 *Sergeant Pepper's Lonely Hearts Club* album.

Leeds Schools Amateur Boxing Association banned boys with Beatles' haircuts from taking part in the city's championships in 1965.

MOTOR RACING MOMENTS

The World Drivers' Championship was won by a British driver six times in the 1960s:

1962 Graham Hill

1963 Jim Clark

1964 John Surtees

1965 Jim Clark

1968 Graham Hill

1969 Jackie Stewart

Surtees achieved his title after winning seven world motorcycling titles – the only man to achieve world titles on two and four wheels. As for farmer Jim Clark, he featured even more heavily in the list of six British Grand Prix winners during this decade, winning in 1962, 1963, 1964, 1965 and 1967. Clark was killed in a crash in a minor race at Hockenheim, Germany, in 1968. The 1969 British Grand Prix was won by Clark's fellow Scot, Jackie Stewart.

Jim Clark was also in the record books as the world's youngest motor racing champion (1963) and as the first non-American to win the Indianapolis 500 in 1965. Staying in America, Graham Hill was the first driver to win the Indianapolis 500 on his debut appearance (May 1966). Two years later, the first three places in the US Grand Prix were taken by the Brits – Jackie Stewart, Graham Hill and John Surtees.

Another British 1-2-3 (and 4) was achieved at the Monte Carlo Rally in 1966 . . . for British cars. However, all four (the first three were all Mini Coopers) were disqualified for having illegal light dipping systems! Home-grown drivers affected were Roger Clark in a Ford Lotus Cortina, originally placed fourth, and Irishman Paddy Hopkirk who was, briefly, third (in one of *The Italian Job* cars). Even Prince Rainier of Monaco declined to attend the prize-giving as was his norm.

When Stirling Moss was banned from driving for a year in April 1960 for dangerous driving, he was still eligible to drive (dangerously?) in Grand Prix races. It was lucky for him as he won the Monaco Grand Prix in May of that year.

BACK TO BALL GAMES – BIG BALLS . . .

During the big freeze of 1963, the Wales v England rugby match looked set to be abandoned, but the Cardiff Arms Park pitch had been protected by 30 tons of straw, which, once cleared, meant play could go ahead – but the grass froze during the game, turning it into an ice-rink, with England winning 13–6. The underground electric heating at Murrayfield meant that the Wales v Scotland match could go ahead in the same freezing conditions – but it was the Welsh who reaped the benefits this time, as they won 6–0.

Scotland were unlucky again against England at Twickenham in 1965. With a minute to go, they were sitting pretty – in the mud – at 3–0 up, but that was when England winger Andy Hancock saved England's bacon with the longest solo run ever seen for a try in an international: at least 95 yards, with some claims for 100.

As for the Irish, there was a riot when the referee failed to notice that Gareth Edwards' drop-kick for Wales (in a 1968 match in Dublin) had missed the goal, something everyone but the referee saw. According to rugby writer and historian John Griffiths, the Irish, now playing at 6–6, were pumped enough to go on to win 9–6, putting an end to the potential for even more riots. Phew!

There is also a story of a rugby match abandoned before it even started – between Colwyn Bay and Porthmadog in 1966 (in North Wales). The rugby ball could not be found anywhere! As a result, both the team and the crowd had no choice but to return home. Bet they remembered to bring a spare next time.

Another pre-match incident was before the start of the 1969 international between the French and Scottish in Paris. Jean-Pierre Salut fell and broke his ankle running up the stairs from the dressing room, apparently blinded by the sun – a variation on the usual type of rugby-related injury with not even a cap to show for his bad luck.

The same year, there was a rugby match between Gloucester and Harlequins, whose Bob Hiller missed an embarrassing eleven goal kicks. Hiller stayed on the pitch when the match ended – to practise. To be fair, he was obviously forgiven because just two months later (December), he captained England for the first time at Twickenham, beating the Springboks for the first time ever.

. . . AND SMALL BALLS

When golfer Tony Jacklin won the Jacksonville Open in 1968, he became the first British golfer to win on US soil for nearly half a century – and he was the first Brit for well over a quarter of a century to win the British Open Championship in 1969 at Royal Lytham.

The only known husband and wife golfers who managed a hole in one at the same hole in the same match (at Turnberry, Scotland, in August 1963) were George and Margaret Gordon – no relation to the author. And one of the few times that a golfer shot his ball into the rough, only to find it being eaten by a cow, was the same year, but in Guernsey. Tasty.

At Wimbledon in the 1960s, the British ladies had much to be loud and proud about. Angela Mortimer beat Christine Truman (another Brit) in July 1961, the first British triumph since 1937. Our Virginia Wade beat the legendary American Billie Jean King in September 1968 in the first US Open Tennis Championships. Ann Jones won Wimbledon in 1969 against three-times-champion Billie Jean King, having lost to her in the 1967 match.

MORE WIMBLEDON

Although the world's oldest amateur tennis tournament, Wimbledon only opened its doors – and nets – to professionals in 1968.

The shortest tennis match recorded at Wimbledon is just 20 minutes – when Susan Tutt beat Marion Bandy 6–0, 6–0 in 1969.

The same year saw the longest ever (then) singles match at Wimbledon between Pancho Gonzales and Charlie Paserell – 41-year old Gonzales won after 112 games which lasted 5 hours and 12 minutes.

SWINGING SIXTIES CRICKET

In cricket in the '60s, Britain did not have an awful lot to shout about – except for Fred Trueman's 300th Test wicket which came against Australia in 1964. Then there was Garfield Sobers' achievement of six sixes in one over in 1968 when captaining Nottingham against Glamorgan at Swansea: another cricket first. Another, lesser-known, batsman who set a world record (that still stands) back in 1965 was Clive Inman. This Sri Lankan batsman who played for Leicestershire scored 50 runs in just 8 minutes at Trent Bridge against Nottinghamshire.

At the other end of the scale was the match between Ross County and Elgin in 1964, when Ross lost one man but had a result which sounded as if they had lost ten – all out for 0 runs.

One golden duck story features British actor, Trevor Howard. A real cricket fan, he got up at 5.00 one morning in 1960 to drive 180 miles to Buxton, Derbyshire, for a game – and was out first ball. He had chosen the right profession, obviously.

Marylebone Cricket Club had a mixed 1960s: they abolished the distinction between amateur and professional cricket, putting an end to the Gentlemen v Players matches. But they failed to select mixed race cricketer Basil D'Oliveira for the 1968 team to play in South Africa (because he was classified there as 'coloured'): white feathers were sent to their offices as a result.

SPORT ON FOUR LEGS

Flat racing jockey Lester Piggott was at the peak of his game in the horse racing world in the 1960s, commencing the decade with his 1,000th winner in 1960. His personal best in one year – 191 winners – came in 1966. As for horsey records, these were down to Arkle, probably the greatest National Hunt horse of all time. He won the Cheltenham Gold Cup in March 1966 for the third time, with a phenomenal lead of 30 lengths, with other wins during the decade including two Hennessey Gold Cups and three wins at the Leopardstown Chase. The third of these was also in 1966, the year of his last race (at Kempton Park) when a leg injury on Boxing Day forced his early retirement. His secret was said to be a daily dose of Guinness.

A famous jockey, a famous horse, and now a famous race: The Grand National. The 1963 race had two claims to fame. First, the barking-mad Spanish aristocrat, the 'Iron' Duke of Albuquerque, made history when bookies offered odds of 66-1 against his finishing in the saddle, thanks to his track record. The unlucky duke fell at the fourth, having booked a private room at the Royal Liverpool Infirmary in anticipation. Secondly, the winner, Ayala, had cost its owner just 40 guineas just four months earlier – not much money, and not much time. In 1967, the 23rd fence, known for unseating so many riders, was christened Foinavon, in honour of the horse of that name who won that year's National at 100-1, having managed to avoid the disaster that was fence 23. The Duchess of Westminster, who owned Arkle and Foinavon, had sold the latter before his historic win because of his poor performance record.

The first time that starting gates were used for horse racing in Britain was at Newmarket in July 1965, and the first race to start that way was the Chesterfield Stakes.

After Florence Nagle had tried for twenty years to get a licence to train horses, Lord Justice Denning finally ruled, in 1966, that there would be equality of the sexes in the world of training. Mind you, Florence was 72 by then, so may have been less than grateful. She had been getting round the problem by using the name of her head lad, so the only difference it made to her was that she was now 'legal'.

Then there were the greyhounds. Mental's Only Hope failed to stop at the end of a race at Wimbledon (March 1961); he just kept going until sheer exhaustion brought him to a halt after over half an hour. Off the track (presumably!) greyhound Low Pressure fathered 2,414 registered puppies and at least 600 unregistered between December 1961 and November 1969. According to the *Guinness Book of Records*, this made him the greatest sire of all time (well, four-legged anyway).

SPORT ON TWO WHEELS

The 1960s were dominated by Mike 'The Bike' Hailwood. He became the first winner of three Isle of Man TT races in one week (1961), took the first of nine world titles for Honda in 1961, became the first rider to win four consecutive 500cc World Championships, and set a lap record in 1967 of 108.77mph at the Isle of Man's Senior TT Race. Hailwood switched from two wheels to four in 1968, including

Formula One racing – until a crash in the '70s.
The first British cyclist to ever wear the prized yellow jersey in the Tour de France, Tommy Simpson from Durham, collapsed and died during the event in 1967 – aged just 29. He had only been a professional rider since 1960, but it seems, with hindsight, that his success was partly attributable to drugs.

BRITS IN THE OLYMPICS

Don Thompson won British gold for the men's 50km walk at the Rome Olympics of 1960. As part of his training, he had to get used to the steamy heat, so had turned up the heating and the hot water taps in his bathroom at home to their highest level. He spent so much time in there that he apparently ran up a bill of £9,000 for eighteen months. No doubt he thought the expenditure was worth it in the end – although, there again, it seems that on his return, he found that the gas board had cut him off! Anita Lonsbrough also did us proud with a gold for the 200m breast stroke. Rome 1960 was the first televised Games.

The first Olympic gold medal ever achieved by a British female athlete – and with a world record – was Mary Rand in the women's long jump (Tokyo 1964 – the first Asian games). She also came through with a creditable silver in the women's pentathlon. This was a good year for British ladies because after Ann Packer won silver in the 400m, she went on to run the 800m as the slowest qualifier. To everyone's astonishment, she not only managed a gold medal, but a world record, too. The men also managed two golds – Ken Matthews in the men's 20km walk, and Lynn 'The Leap' Davies in the men's long jump. Tokyo 1964 was the first Olympics to be televised in colour.

Great Britain managed one gold at the Winter Olympics that took place in the '60s: at Innsbrück, in 1964, where snow and ice had to be transported from the mountain tops by the Austrian army because of a drastic shortage on the ground. The two-man bobsleigh team of Tony Nash and Robin Dixon were the first ever 'lowland' team to win the event.

When David Hemery won gold (and broke the world record) in the 1968 Summer Olympic Games in Mexico City for the 400m hurdles, over-excited commentator David Coleman declared 'Hemery first, Hennige [Germany] second, who cares who's third?' John Sherwood cared – he was the Brit who won the bronze. Whoops! Other gold medallists who flew the flag for Great Britain in 1968 included Rodney Pattisson and Iain Macdonald-Smith for Flying Dutchman yachting in their racing dinghy called *Supercalifragilisticexpialidocious*! This was particularly impressive because they had been disqualified in their first race (but won five of the next six). Then there was Chris Finnegan for middleweight boxing, our first boxing medal for twelve years (with 32 years before there was another). Vet Bob Braithwaite's gold for clay pigeon shooting was even more remarkable, perhaps, as the first Brit to win the event for 44 years. Finally, there was the three-day event team's gold. These were the first Olympics to be seriously affected by politics, especially with regard to the demonstrations of Black Power openly exhibited.

OLYMPIANS WORLDWIDE . . .

In 1960, Crown Prince (later King) Constantine of Greece won a sailing gold medal in the Dragon class. Other royal Princes, Harald of Norway (1964 and 1968) and Bira of Thailand (1964), also competed in sailing events, but did not match the Greek's achievement.

Hungarian fencer Aladar Gerevich won his seventh gold medal in 1960, although the Hungarian Fencing Committee had felt he was 'too old' at 50 to compete. To convince them, he had challenged the entire sabre team to individual matches during the trials, and won every match. Old? Old? Less successful that year was Wym Essajas of Dutch Guiana (now Suriname) who should have made history as the first to represent his country. But, and it's a big but, he had been told that the 800m heats were taking place in the afternoon, when in fact they happened in the morning while he was resting. Oh dear. Just goes to prove the importance of double-checking, and triple-checking, and the rest.

Although the Australian swimmer Dawn Fraser won gold medals in the 1960 and 1964 Olympics to add to her tally from the '50s, she was banned for ten years from 1964 (the year she became Australian of the Year!) because her celebrations included 'acquiring' the national flag from the Japanese Imperial Palace. Severe retribution indeed. Even more severe, but rather more deserved, was the ban for life meted out to Spanish featherweight boxer Valentin Loren who, after being disqualified in the first round of his match against his Formosan opponent (also 1964), delivered the punch of the match – at the referee.

Swedish yachtsmen Stig Lennart Kall and Lars Gunnar Kall missed out on a gold medal in 1964 because they stopped to rescue two sailors whose boat had sunk. Gold? Who needs it? They did win the first Fair Play prize, though, awarded by the International Olympic Committee. Fellow countryman Sture Pettersson, who finished just 0.16 seconds behind the gold medallist in the individual cycling road race that year, must have thought he was in with the chance of a medal – but, because of the great pack of riders who finished together, he was placed 52nd!

The first person to win a marathon twice was Abebe Bikila – in Rome, 1960, when he became the first Ethiopian to win a gold (barefoot), and again at Tokyo in 1964, setting a new record – with shoes. Abebe, when not running, was an imperial bodyguard to Emperor Haile Selassie.

To set a world record in the long jump, you only need an extra centimetre – but Bob Beamon from the US beat the previous record by 55cm in 1968 – with his first jump of 8.9m, a staggering 71cm ahead of the silver medallist. The length of the jump meant that a new tape measure had to be introduced! His record stood for twenty-three years.

Also in 1968, but at the Winter Olympics in Grenoble, three of the women competing in the luge for East Germany were disqualified for heating the runners on their sled to make it go faster on the ice. This was the first time East Germany had entered as a separate team – not a good start.

The first official Paralympics were held in Rome in 1960, with every British competitor who entered (31 entries, the highest of any country except Italy) winning a medal including 20 golds. Just as remarkable was the individual achievement of ten medals won in 1968 by Roberto Marson from Italy. He won three gold medals in field athletics, three in swimming (beating the two golds he'd won in 1964) and four in fencing. An all-rounder by anyone's standards. The 1968 Paralympics were held in Tel Aviv, as there were difficulties with the Mexico City facilities.

FIVE FINAL (OLYMPIAN) FACTS

In Rome in 1960, Pope John had the best seat for canoeing as he could watch it from the balcony of his summer residence.

The first purpose-built Winter Games venue was opened by President Nixon at Squaw Valley in the USA in 1960, with an opening ceremony directed by none other than Walt Disney.

South Africa was banned from the Olympics from 1964 (until 1992) because of their apartheid policy; nor did they appear in any Winter Olympics between 1960 and 1994.

In the cat-and-mouse tactics employed in the cycling 'sprint', the duo (Pettenela of Italy and Trentin of France) involved in the 1964 semi-final set up a truly bizarre record – both standing still for 21 minutes and 57 seconds!

The first International Special Olympics Summer Games were held in Chicago in 1968 (for those with learning disabilities), thanks to Eunice Kennedy Shriver, President Kennedy's sister. Another sister, Rosemary, had suffered brain damage following an operation. As a result, Eunice became the only woman to subsequently have her portrait appear on a US coin in her lifetime.

IS YOUR SPORT HERE?

The walking race from John O'Groats to Land's End was set up in 1960 by holiday camp king, Billy Butlin. He offered prize money totalling some £5,500 to the first woman and man to finish, plus runners-up prizes. It started on a snowy February day, not the best of times, and of the 1,200 entries, only between 113 and 138 finished (reports vary) with around 100 disqualified for cheating – by accepting lifts! James 'Little Jim' Musgrave was the eventual winner over 1,000 miles later in Land's End after 15 days, 14 hours and 31 minutes.

British chess championships in the 1960s were dominated by Jonathan Penrose. He was awarded the International Masters Title in 1961 and won the British championship every year of the decade except 1964/5.

Mountain climbing? Chris Bonington and Ian Clough became the first Brits to conquer the north face of the Eiger in August 1962, and Mike Burke and Dougal Haston were the first up the north face of the comparably daunting Matterhorn in winter – February 1967.

The first British outdoor artificial ski slope was inspired by the harsh winter of 1962/1963 when skiers on the Torbay hills in Devon had become hooked on the sport. Fred Pontin (another holiday camp king) provided a suitable site in the grounds of his Barton Hall holiday complex, but doubled its size, and turned up for the opening ceremony in 1963 in his private helicopter.

BBC SPORTS PERSONALITIES OF THE YEAR

1960 David Broome, showjumper (bronze medallist, 1960 Olympics)

1961 Stirling Moss

1962 Anita Lonsbrough (the first woman to win the award)

1963 Dorothy Hyman (100m and 200m gold at the 1962 Commonwealth Games)

1964 Mary Rand (three in a row for the ladies)

1965 Tommy Simpson

1966 Bobby Moore (of course)

1967 Henry Cooper

1968 David Hemery

1969 Ann Jones

TWO BRITS IN AMERICA – WITH DIVERSE RESULTS

When Briton Gerry Carr (a former discus champion) took part in a relay race in Los Angeles in 1962, he grabbed the baton so hard that it broke. Carr had set a number of British discus records in the '60s becoming No. 1 in the British all-time top ten discus throwers in 1965, so his grip was arguably stronger than most.

Distance runner Bruce Tulloh of Britain set a number of European records between 1965 and 1967, in bare feet, but then retired from international competition. However, he went on to compete in the 2,830-mile run from Los Angeles to New York in 1969. Not only compete, but win, setting a new record of 64 days 22 hours, eight days faster than the previous record.

AND AN AMERICAN IN BRITAIN

Fred Baldasare from the US became the first person to swim the English Channel underwater – without surfacing – in July 1962. OK, OK, so he was aided by scuba equipment, but this didn't stop him making it into the *Guinness Book of Records*, and *Ripley's Believe it or Not*.

9

LITERATURE, ART & THE STAGE

THE CHANGING NOVEL

Barbara Cartland was the unchanging face of the novel. She published her 100th romance in 1963, and, by 1969, was still selling over a million paperbacks every year. The American author, Jacqueline Susann, found a different way of achieving impressive sales. When her second novel, *Valley of the Dolls*, was published in 1966, she was said to have bought up large quantities from the bookstores that the *New York Times* used to determine their listings, and that did the trick: she went to No. 1 on their bestseller list, justifying her heavy expenditure.

It wasn't just Americans who could do raunchy. When Penguin, who published *Lady Chatterley's Lover* in 1960 after a thirty-year ban, were prosecuted under the new Obscene Publications Act, there were over seventy witnesses in its defence, including the Bishop of Woolwich. The jury had been instructed to read D.H. Lawrence's novel before the trial, and, after three hours, they declared that the material was not obscene. Unsurprisingly, Penguin sold 200,000 copies the next day, and the book went on to sell 4 million copies. There was one (tongue in cheek?) review in *Field and Stream* in 1961 who felt readers were better suited to read *Practical Gamekeeping* than *Lady Chatterley* because to glean the details of the life of an English gamekeeper, readers were obliged to 'wade through many pages of extraneous material'. John Cleland's *Fanny Hill* suffered a worse fate when released in 'an unexpurgated edition' in 1964 (two hundred years after the original expurgated version) – Bow Street magistrates ordered that all copies should be seized and the ban stayed in place until 1970.

The changes in class and culture taking place had a real influence on the publishing industry from the late 1950s. Kitchen sink dramas were not restricted to the screen – they were also in book form, and of course many such screenings were based on successful books. Working in reverse, *Cathy Come Home* by Jeremy Sandford (an old Etonian) was published in 1967 after its powerful screening as part of the *Wednesday Play* series. Sandford's first wife, Nell Dunn (the daughter of a millionaire), published *Up the Junction* in 1963 (more non-fiction than novel, and published before its television appearance) and *Poor Cow* in 1967, which became a successful film. The books offered powerful insights into the working class even though written by, effectively, 'outsiders'. Stan Barstow had similar success with *A Kind of Loving* (1960) which took the kitchen sink up north, but his own roots (a coal-miner father) were less surprising.

Anti-heroes arrived with books like Kingsley Amis's *Take A Girl Like You* in 1960 and the American Joseph Heller's wartime satire *Catch-22* in 1961. These were published alongside more conventional heroic exploits with James Bond novels still featuring up to and after Ian Fleming's death in 1964. It is documented that sales of the Bond novels in the USA shot up dramatically from 1961 onwards, after President Kennedy included *From Russia With Love* on a list of his favourite books.

FOUR FICTIONAL FIRSTS

John Lennon published his first work (stories, verse, cartoons) in 1964 – *In His Own Write* – described within as his 'correction of short writty' [*sic*] but outsold by *Fanny Cradock's Daily Telegraph Cook Book*.

France's Jean-Paul Sartre rejected the Nobel Prize for Literature in 1964 – the first to do so, although others had wobbled – because it would 'lessen the impact' of his work and make him 'institutionalised'.

The Booker Prize for the best British work of fiction was introduced in 1969, and the first winner was Peter Newby, a BBC radio executive, with *Something to Answer For*. At this stage, there was no ceremony – he got a letter in the post.

The first novel published without using the letter e (the question why? springs to mind) was in 1969 by Georges Perec, another Frenchman: perhaps that explains it. If you want to read it, it's called *La Disparition* (or *The Disappearance* – of the e perhaps) or, in translation, *The Void*. Gorgs Prc does not have the same ring, somehow.

A COUPLE OF SURPRISES

In 1963, Lord Denning's *Official Report on the Profumo Affair* went on sale in London. It became one of the year's best sellers, with as many as 100,000 copies sold in the first 24 hours alone. It was described at the time as the 'raciest and most readable Blue Book' – Blue! – that had ever been published – and is still available, on Amazon.

Three years later, the publication of *Quotations from the Works of Mao Tse-Tung* became second only to the Bible in non-fiction sales. (Assuming the Bible is non-fiction, of course).

BORROWED BOOKS

Ten-year-old Andrew Wiles borrowed a book about Fermat's Last Theorem from his local library in Cambridge in 1963, and made it his life's ambition to prove what no statistician before him had been able to prove. And, yes, reader, he managed it – though it took him the next thirty years.

Boots Booklovers' Library, which had been operating since the nineteenth century, lending books from the branches of the chemist's for a subscription of a few pence per week, bought up W.H. Smith's rival business in 1961, a tad optimistically. Due to the increased availability of cheap paperbacks, and the 'free' national library service, Boots Booklovers' Libraries finally closed in 1966.

For several years in the 1960s, Joe Orton (the playwright) and his friend Kenneth Halliwell got away with defacing a wide range of library books that they borrowed (surreptitiously) from Islington Library. They altered blurbs and defaced covers – most examples too crude to reproduce here, but, as a taster, one of the *Collected Plays of Emlyn Williams* was retitled *Knickers Must Fall*. These were shock tactics in apparent protest at the limited availability of books on offer, with the added offence of pages from art books torn out to paper their walls. As a result, they both spent six months in prison.

THE GROWTH IN CHOICES FOR CHILDREN

It was no longer just about Enid Blyton – although hundreds of her books were still published in the 1960s. However, the last of the Secret Seven and Famous Five books were published in 1963, and the last Noddy book was released in 1964 (Noddy had already sold well over 26 million books by then). Of the male writers for children, her contemporary, the prolific Frank Richards, author of the Billy Bunter books, died in 1961. The last of these, *Bunter's Last Fling*, was published in 1965 – with some help from other writers, for obvious reasons. Writer Roald Dahl took over their mantle to some extent, his success kicking off with *James and the Giant Peach* and *Charlie and the Chocolate Factory* (1961 and 1964 respectively) although *Gremlins* had been written nearly twenty years earlier. The Oompa Loompas in *Charlie*, incidentally, started out as black pygmies from Africa but, following accusations in some quarters of racism and slavery, were amended in later editions.

Of the sixty books published by the American 'Dr' (he wasn't!) Seuss, eleven were released in the 1960s, the most enduring of these being *Green Eggs and Ham* – that he apparently produced after being challenged to write a book in just 50 words.

BIRTHS (NEWSPAPERS, MAGAZINES AND COMICS)

1960 *Buster* launched with free 'balloon bleeper' (a whistling balloon, and why not) in every copy of the first issue – the start of a long run.

Honey was one of the first 'Swinging Sixties' teenage magazines, and one of the earliest monthlies of its kind.

Judy joined its established and popular stable-mate *Bunty* (for pre-teenage girls).

1961 The *Sunday Telegraph* arrived – a sister for the *Daily Telegraph*.

Private Eye (fortnightly satire) appeared, with subscribers ranging from Lady Violet Bonham Carter to inmates of HM Prisons. The first issue was produced on a manual typewriter with pages pasted with Cow Gum! W.H. Smith refused to stock it – the paper, not the Cow Gum.

The Victor arrived for schoolboys.

1962 *Sunday Times Colour Supplement*, the first of its kind (with Jean Shrimpton on the cover and Mary Quant within its pages).

Spiderman arrived in an American comic called *Amazing Fantasy* (and a copy of this issue sold in recent years in the US for over a million dollars). A year later, the character had his own comic: *The Amazing Spiderman*.

Look and Learn, an educational magazine, launched with the Prince of Wales perhaps not an obvious choice for the first cover – but with a successful large and colourful format.

1964 The *Sun* rose, the first national for over 30 years; becoming a tabloid in 1969.

Rave, Fabulous, Ready Steady Go and *Jackie* took on the teenage market, with their emphasis on pop music and pop stars.

1965 *Nova* magazine launched – for 'feminists', 'radicals', 'intellectuals' and the 'sophisticated'.

The first British *Penthouse* arrived to ensure that the male market was, er, covered.

1966 The *International Times*, Britain's first alternative newspaper, was launched at the 'groovy' Roundhouse in London – but had a short life.

Petticoat arrived (a boom decade for teenage magazines).

Another glamour magazine to rival *Penthouse* (and *Playboy*, which had been around since the '50s) arrived: *Mayfair*.

Oz took on the Establishment, with 'Turn on, Tune in and Drop dead'. *Rolling Stone* started out in the US with John Lennon on the cover. It was named after the Muddy Waters' song, not the British band.

Time Out listings magazine started out on a budget of £75, which may explain why there were just eight pages in its first issue.

TV Times launched nationally (previously it had regional variants).

19 – yet another teenage mag launched.

DEATHS (NEWSPAPERS, MAGAZINES AND COMICS)

1960 The *Sunday Empire News* (incorporated into the *News of the World*).

The *News Chronicle* (ditto the *Daily Mail*).

The *Star* could no longer compete with its rival, the *London Evening News*.

The end of the *Sunday Graphic*.

1961 The *Sunday Dispatch* gave up competing with the *Sunday Express*.

1963 *Marty* (based on the popularity of pop star Marty Wilde) merged with *Mirabelle*, after three years.

Two more teenage magazines featuring the very British genre of love-stories-in-pictures, *Roxy* and *Serenade*, merged with *Valentine*, the latter after just 25 issues.

1964 The end of the *Daily Herald* (forerunner of the *Sun*).
Popular 1950s comic, *Girl*, merged with *Princess* (which had been around for only four years), with another merger in 1967 (with *Tina*) resulting in . . . *Princess Tina* (a time of change, obviously).

1965 *Marilyn* was another that merged with *Valentine* although the venues for romance within its pages didn't change – coffee bars, discos, the seaside or pop festivals, the office . . . certainly no foreign travel was involved.
The *West Indian Gazette*, Britain's first 'black' newspaper, folded after death of its founder.
The *Children's Newspaper* merged with *Look and Learn* after nearly 2,500 issues.
School Friend merged with *June* (which had started out in 1961).

1966 The comic *Ranger* also merged with *Look and Learn*.

1967 The end of the *Sunday Citizen* and, in complete contrast, the merger of *Boyfriend* with *Petticoat*.

1969 *Eagle* (complete with Dan Dare) merged with another I.P.C. boys' comic, *Lion*.

LOOKING INSIDE – AND BEHIND – THE PAGES

In June 1962, a mini version of the *Radio Times* was produced, just 7.5cm x 6cm, for the royal dolls' house.

The *Commonwealth Sentinel* has gone on record as our shortest-lived newspaper although it described itself as 'Britain's most fearless newspaper'. It launched in London on 6 February 1965 but the founder had omitted to organise any distribution – and 50,000 copies were dumped outside Brown's Hotel where he was staying. The police got involved because the newspapers were blocking the street, and, in the end, just one copy was sold, to an interested passer-by. No further 'fearless' copies were forthcoming.

According to *The Guinness Book of Records*, the biggest newspaper in history – with 946 pages and weighing 7½lb – was published on 17 October 1965. It was the *New York (Sunday) Times*.

When Lord Thomson bought *The Times* (September 1966), one journalist said that this proved that the 'freedom of the press is for he who owns one'. He promptly changed its front page for the first time in its history from a page of advertisements to include news stories and pictures.

After spending the day working as a sub-editor on *Queen* magazine in the early '60s, John Betjeman's daughter (Candida) would toddle over to the *Private Eye* offices to help staple copies together and did her bit to persuade friends to subscribe. The editor of *Queen* saw this as moonlighting and sacked her. Lacking a sense of humour perhaps?

In April 1966, America's *Time* magazine declared London the 'City of the Decade' and spawned the phrase we made our own: 'Swinging London'.

In 1967, *The Times* carried a full-page advertisement advocating the legalisation of marijuana – signed by such notables as all four Beatles (who seemingly also financed the page). Well, they would.

Hugh Hefner (the man behind *Playboy* magazine and clubs) spread his moral wings in the '60s and managed to increase the number of subscriptions from the clergy by offering them a 25 per cent discount! When seminarians (theology students) complained, he extended the offer to them. Note that both the Revd Jesse Jackson and Martin Luther King featured – though not as models – in '60s editions of *Playboy*.

The *Daily Mirror* launched its supplement, Mirrorscope, in January 1968 – advising the working man how to invest his spare cash – but the average reader did not seem to have that much spare cash to invest so it fizzled out after a few years.

WHAT WAS HAPPENING IN POETRY?

Well, more than 6,500 people attended a poetry reading at the Royal Albert Hall in London in 1965 after it got a mention on the BBC. The American Allen Ginsberg was one of the modern 'beat poets' in attendance – and many were seemingly stoned, chanting, singing and smoking. It attracted people who had not attended a reading before – or since, perhaps.

Performance poetry was personified during this decade by the androgynous Stevie Smith, although her most famous poem (*Not*

Waving But Drowning) dates from the 1950s. The eccentric off-key presentation of her work became very popular, and she was awarded the Queen's Gold Medal for Poetry in 1969. American poet Sylvia Plath was apparently a fan and made an appointment to meet her but committed suicide before the meeting.

Sylvia Plath had her first collection, *Colossus,* published in 1960, but her second, *Ariel* (1965) was published two years after she committed suicide. Her husband (ex-husband at the time of her death), Ted Hughes, also had two collections of poetry published in the '60s, but went on producing award-winning work for many more decades. In 1961, he won the oldest prize in British literature – the Hawthornden – for *Lupercal.*

Poet John 'I must go down to the seas again' Masefield died in 1967 (of gangrene) a month short of his 89th birthday after thirty-seven years as Poet Laureate. He was the longest-serving Poet Laureate since Lord Tennyson (1850–92). Cecil Day Lewis, the father of actor Daniel Day Lewis, took over the mantle – not just a poet, but a crime novelist, too.

Whitsun Weddings (1964) was arguably Philip Larkin's tour de force and his only collection of the decade, leading to a Fellowship of the Royal Society of Literature and the 1965 Queen's Gold Medal for Poetry. Although, ironically, he never married, he was kept very busy as Hull's most famous librarian and as a jazz critic for the *Daily Telegraph.*

John Betjeman was knighted in 1969 (having won the Queen's Gold Medal in 1960, the year he received a CBE) but made his name at the time not just from his poetry but from the documentaries and travelogues he made for the BBC as well as for British Transport Films and some of ITV's regional stations. These, and other 'guest' appearances on television, served to reinforce not only his high public profile, but offered a platform for his known nostalgic interests in architecture, in the preservation of the railways and Victoriana. *Summoned by Bells*, his autobiography in verse, was a best-seller on publication in 1960.

OP ART AND POP ART

Although not new to the '60s, both of these art forms really took off during the decade to keep pace with the revolution in popular culture, both in Britain and the US.

Op Art uses optical illusions to create an image, with Bridget Riley perhaps the most well-known British proponent, especially with regard to her early monochrome images, synonymous with hallucinatory drug experiences. In 1965, she tried, unsuccessfully, to sue an American dressmaker for copying her op art designs, preferring to see them on canvas than on people, which 'vulgarised' them. Bridget Riley was the first woman to win the International Prize for Painting (Venice), in 1969.

Pop Art – using images from popular culture such as soup tins and comic strip drawings – had a number of British artists as central figures in the 1960s, principally Derek Boshier and David Hockney. Boshier achieved fame in part for his 1962 collage featuring Buddy Holly and Lord Nelson (*I Wonder What My Heroes Think of The Space Race),* which hung for a while in the Moscow Gallery; Hockney's '60s paintings favoured swimming pools – and fit young men. Their American contemporaries Roy Lichtenstein and Andy Warhol produced their own distinctive works in the genre, notably *Whaam* (1963) and the *Marilyn Diptych* (1962) respectively. Such works have been reproduced not only on clothes but on mugs, tea-towels, postcards . . . and why not.

ANECDOTAL ART

Jacob Epstein's last major work of sculpture was unveiled at Coventry Cathedral in June 1960, a year after his death. *St Michael and the Devil* now occupies a prominent position, but the choice of sculptor was initially viewed with some suspicion because Epstein was a Jew, until someone pointed out that so was Jesus.

The Chinese Girl by Vladimir Tretchikoff was turned into an art print in 1960 and sold in its millions. Sometimes known as *The Green Lady*, it adorned such walls as Ruby's flat in *Alfie*. As for the artist, he had an exhibition at Harrods in 1961 attended by 205,000 people and became one of the most commercially successful artists of all time, proud to display his success with such trappings as his pink cadillac.

Goya's famous portrait of the Duke of Wellington was stolen from the National Gallery in 1961 and returned four years later. In the meantime, it turned up in Dr No's dining room in the 1962 Bond film.

In 1961, Henri Matisse's *Le Bateau* (The Boat – painted with its reflection in the water) was hung upside down for 47 days in the Museum of Modern Art in New York before anyone noticed. Bet that produced a few red faces.

In January 1963, French artist Robert Filliou announced that art had started exactly one million years ago when someone dropped a sponge into a bucket of water and saw the result. He proposed an annual public holiday to celebrate the event – but, sadly, no one was listening.

In Düsseldorf in 1965, a German artist called Joseph Beuys stuck honey and gold leaf on his head, attached a ski-like slab of iron to one foot (to produce some sound as he moved), and proceeded to 'explain' the pictures in the gallery to a dead hare. He was trying a theatrical method of demonstrating how it is possible to fail to communicate. Certainly worked.

The eccentric Salvador Dali – he of the twirling moustache and pet ocelot – gifted a drawing of a crucifix to Riker's Island Jail in New York in 1965 as part of the Art in Prison programme. It took pride of place in their dining hall. Wonder if they knew that he had completed it in an hour in his New York hotel . . . ?

Yoko Ono staged her 'Half a Wind' show in London's Lisson Gallery in 1967, with John Lennon's financial support, incorporating 'Half a Room' showing halves of everyday objects (bed, chair, teapot – even a cake) painted white. Subtitled 'Yoko Plus Me', this seemed to suggest that the twosome were two halves of the same, or yin and yang. A year later, Lennon and Ono presented Coventry Cathedral with a white wrought iron bench slotted together around two acorns (one planted East, and one West) intended to grow inside the bench – part of their Acorns for Peace tour. Less peaceful was the argument over the positioning of the bench, and the prompt theft of acorns and identifying plaque which read 'Yoko by John, John by Yoko'. Lennon and Ono had met at the Indica Gallery in London in 1966 when she was preparing her exhibition 'Unfinished Paintings and Objects'.

ON STAGE

When Lionel Bart's *Oliver!* opened in June 1960 at the New Theatre, London, it became the first hugely successful British musical (previous hits had all been American imports). Bart, who could neither read nor write music, claims that he developed the score by using some of Mozart's music, backwards, then added the words. The show ran for six years and three months, making it the longest-running musical in the West End at the time. Bart's *Blitz* and *Maggie May* achieved similar success from 1962 and 1964 respectively in the West End, running for over 500 performances, but *Twang* (1965) was a resounding flop.

Beyond the Fringe opened at the Fortune Theatre, London, in May 1961 after its launch at the 1960 Edinburgh Festival, with Peter Cook, Dudley Moore, Alan Bennett and Jonathan Miller popularising a new combination of revue and satire. However, *The Sound of Music*, which opened the same year at London's Palace Theatre, probably filled more seats.

Also in 1961, *The Mousetrap* (which had already been running for nine years) was the first play to be advertised on a cricket scorecard (at Lord's). The actor David Raven, who played Major Metcalf, went on to achieve, by 1967, the longest engagement by any stage actor in the world in one role. Incidentally, Christie's last West End play, *Rule of Three*, opened in 1962 at the Duchess Theatre.

Another record-breaker was the un-p.c. *Black and White Minstrel Show* which featured in the *Guinness Book of Records* as the show seen by the most people. It ran at the Victoria Palace from 1962 (after fifteen years of *The Crazy Gang*) to 1972, twice nightly, with nearly 8,000,000 tickets sold. Even the West Indies cricket team bought tickets when on tour.

The Theatre Royal at Stratford East continued its 1950s experimentation with improvisation, with cockney actors rather than trained thespians, with working class drama and working class subjects. In 1963, Joan Littlewood and her Theatre Workshop Company in the East End had their biggest success – *Oh! What a Lovely War,* which went on to do well not only in the West End but on Broadway and on the big screen. Littlewood's military advisor for this production, Raymond Fletcher, who had served as a politician as well as in the forces, was later revealed to have been a spy. *Sparrers Can't Sing* and *A Taste of Honey* were also popular 1960s films that originated on the stage of the Theatre Royal.

Returning to a more conventional arena, The National Theatre (the company) had their opening night in October 1963 at the Old Vic, with *Hamlet* featuring Peter O'Toole, directed by Laurence Olivier, with Frank Finlay as 'First Grave-digger' – regarded by reviewers as an Elizabethan *Look Back in Anger*. The National Theatre (the building) finally started to take shape on the South Bank in London in 1969, although the planning had started in 1951. It is, confusingly, actually not one but three theatres.

For something a bit different on the stage, London, again, had something to offer when Danny La Rue opened his own nightclub in Hanover Square in 1964 after years of panto and cabaret. Danny, who went on to become the most famous female impersonator in the world, attracted over 13,000 members and fans included Noel Coward, Judy Garland, Lord Snowdon and Princess Margaret. Much of his stage material was written by Barry Cryer, and his straight man in those days was half his height (in heels, that is) – his name? Ronnie Corbett.

The Windmill Theatre – and the Windmill girls – gave their farewell performance in October 1964 after thirty-two years. This had been the only theatre in the world where the first six rows of the seats had to be resecured to the floor every morning after the rush for, and subsequent ill-treatment of, the seats the night before when everyone had tried to get a close-up view of the flesh on the stage!

This may surprise some people. The star who appeared at the London Palladium in 1965 for 42 weeks – a run which broke all box office records, and resulted in a Variety Club Award – was . . . Ken Dodd. He set another record soon after which featured in the 1967 *Guinness Book of Records* – for the longest joke-telling session: 1,500 jokes in 3½ hours, i.e. over seven jokes per minute. What a laugh!

When Edward Bond's *Saved* appeared at the Royal Court Theatre, London, in 1965, the controversial stoning-the-baby-in-the-pram scene caused uproar among critics and audiences, and a criminal charge. A sympathetic magistrate handed out a paltry £50 fine – and this play has been credited with assisting in eradicating censorship on the stage (which finally happened in 1968).

Judi Dench may have joined the Royal Shakespeare Company in 1961, but in 1968 she put on a very different hat – and heels - when she took on the hit role of Sally Bowles in the first London production of *Cabaret* at the Palace Theatre.

Marianne Faithfull played Ophelia (and was described by at least one reviewer as 'not convincingly virginal') to Nicol Williamson's very convincing *Hamlet* in 1968 – at hip venue the Roundhouse in North London, a role for which he received the Evening Standard Best Actor Award (having received the same award only five years earlier for *Inadmissible Evidence*).

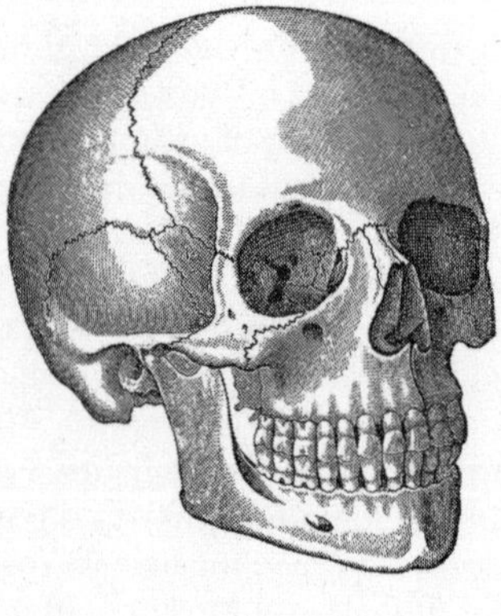

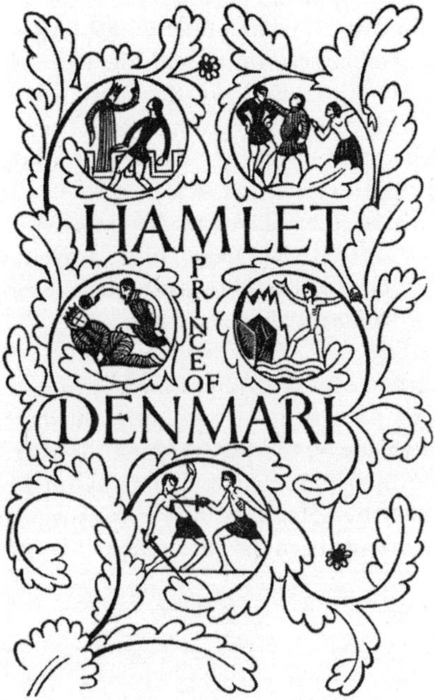

When hippy musical *Hair* opened in 1968 (with newbies Paul Nicholas, Marsha Hunt, Elaine Paige, Oliver Tobias and Tim Curry) two days after the abolition of censorship, it opened to a packed house and encouraged audience participation in the dancing (and the nudity) at the end of the show. Among those joining in on stage were Zsa Zsa Gabor and . . . the Duke of Bedford. Princess Anne also joined in at a 1969 performance, though not with the nudity.

TIPPY TOES AND TOP NOTES

While the Cold War rumbled on and spies were defecting left, right, and centre, one name stood out in the 1960s. Not a spy, not a politician or a subversive writer, but a ballet dancer – Rudolf Nureyev. After being ordered by Russian Embassy officials to return to Moscow, and not to fly to London from France with the rest of the Leningrad Ballet, he dashed through a security barrier appealing for his freedom. After temporary asylum in France (June 1961) – during which time he signed up with the Grand Ballet du Marquis de Cuevas – he settled in the West. His first duet with Margot Fonteyn was in *Giselle* when he was a guest artiste with the Royal Ballet (at Covent Garden) in February 1962. By 1964, they were in the *Guinness Book of Records* for the greatest recorded number of curtain calls received by ballet dancers – 89 to be precise – in October of that year, for their performance in *Swan Lake*. In 1965, in spite of the age difference (she was 45 to his 26) they played the lovers in the opening night of *Romeo and Juliet* at the Royal Opera House, Covent Garden, and the response was sufficient not only to send them touring the US but to perform on the *Ed Sullivan Show*.

The Covent Garden Opera Company was granted the title of the Royal Opera Company in 1968 – only the third stage company to be honoured in this way, the others being the Royal Ballet (in the 1950s) and the Royal Shakespeare Company (in 1961). The Royal Shakespeare Theatre in Stratford-upon-Avon was also renamed in 1961, having previously been the Shakespeare Memorial Theatre.

10

IN THE NEWS

NEW PLACES

Butlin's at Bognor Regis opened in 1960, followed by Minehead (complete with innovative monorail) in 1962, and Barry in 1966. By then, the chalets had hot running water, and were latterly introduced to the option of self-catering as well as the original full board – Billy Butlin was trying hard to compete with the new attraction of foreign holidays but the lure of the holiday camp was in decline by the end of the 1960s.

An ambitious inner-city development was completed in 1961 in Sheffield. Park Hill's 17 acres and 1,000 flats served as a gateway to the town, inspired by French designer Le Corbusier. In an attempt to preserve the community ideal, neighbours were rehoused in close proximity, cobbles from the demolished terraces were reused, and so were original street names. The complex is now the largest Grade II listing in the country – although the highest proportion of post-war listed buildings are churches, because more churches were built in the 1960s than any decade in a century.

The London Hilton in Park Lane opened in 1963, with 512 rooms on 28 floors reaching over 100 metres, giving spectacular views over the London skyline.

The Royal Festival Hall in London reopened in 1965 after a refit and work began on two adjacent concert halls on the South Bank. The Queen Elizabeth Hall was opened in 1967 by, fittingly, Her Majesty the Queen, and the smaller Purcell Room opened just two days later.

The first Playboy Club in Europe opened at 45 Park Lane in 1966 over six floors, with 100 Playboy bunnies in attendance, following the legalisation of gambling. It was to become known as the Hutch on the Park. Hugh Hefner, brought up in a strict Methodist home, opened his first in Chicago in February 1960.

In marked contrast, the Trellick Tower in Notting Hill was designed in 1966 for the Greater London Council (although not completed till the early '70s). Each of the 217 flats was a duplex, based on the design of railway carriages by Erno Goldfinger. Its 31 storeys and separate lift tower have been listed, perhaps bravely, given that much venom has been sent its way – one such 'anti' was the author Ian Fleming, hence his creation of *Goldfinger* as a villain. 400 high-rise buildings were built in London after the Labour Government introduced generous grants to fund such building programmes.

Billy Butlin turns up again in 1966 when he was at the opening in May (to the public) of the rotating restaurant and viewing galleries at the top of the Post Office Tower in London. It was officially opened by Harold Wilson in October 1965, and was then the tallest building in Britain at over 620ft (including the radio mast). Why Billy Butlin? Because he had leased the restaurant.

Liverpool's Grade II listed ultra-modern Catholic Cathedral opened in April 1967 after five years in the construction. Although its official title is the Metropolitan Cathedral Church of Christ the King, it has not one but two nicknames: The Mersey Funnel or Paddy's Wigwam, both references to its conical shape! Each year the Liverpool Beer Festival is held in its crypt, for devotees of a different kind.

These were the 'new towns' designated in the 1960s, around a historic core, to allow for housing shortfalls and new post-war developments:

Skelmersdale and Livingston in 1962
Telford in 1963
Runcorn, Washington (Tyne & Wear) and Redditch in 1964
Irvine in 1966
Newtown (Powys) and Milton Keynes in 1967
Peterborough, Warrington and Northampton in 1968

ALL CHANGE IN POLITICS

Harold Macmillan, plagued by the Profumo scandal, was replaced by Sir Alec Douglas-Home as the Conservative Prime Minister in 1963. As a result, Douglas-Home became the first person to resign a peerage (Earl of Home) to take on the role. This did not seem to impress the British public, however, because just one year later Harold Wilson became the first Labour Prime Minister for thirteen years, staying in office until 1970 (his first term). 48-year-old Wilson, the youngest British Prime Minister of the twentieth century at the time, secured the 1964 election with the narrowest victory in the history of party politics. When asked if he felt like a Prime Minister, his response was 'I feel like a drink'. He did much better in 1966, however, when the General Election re-elected him with the second largest majority in Labour's history. No doubt he still needed a drink, though.

Another MP who renounced his peerage (in August 1963) was Anthony Wedgwood Benn, Viscount Stansgate, following the Peerage Act (in which he was instrumental).

The new Tory leader from 1965, replacing Douglas-Home, was Edward Heath, the youngest since Disraeli and, rarely, a 'commoner' and a bachelor.

When David Steel won a by-election (Roxburgh, Selkirk and Peebles) for the Liberals in 1965, he became the youngest MP in Britain at the age of 26.

Another David, Labour's Plymouth MP, Dr David Owen, became the youngest in the Government when appointed Under-Secretary of State for the Navy in 1968, aged 30.

Irish Republican activist Bernadette Devlin took over the mantle of 'youngest ever British MP' and 'the youngest woman ever elected to the British House of Commons' in April 1969 when elected to the

British Parliament from Northern Ireland at just 21 years of age. She was arrested barely four months later during the Battle of the Bogside, opposing the British occupation of Northern Ireland, and spent four months in prison the following year, while still an MP.

The youngest Conservative female MP in a government role in 1961 (under Macmillan) was one Margaret Thatcher, whose first post at age 36 was as Parliamentary Under-Secretary at the Ministry of Pensions and National Insurance. She was the first female MP to sponsor an Act through Parliament – the Public Bodies (Admission to Meetings) Act of 1960, extending the rights of the Public and the Press (equating with more transparency), resulting, obviously, in her maiden speech.

SOME 'FIRSTS' IN SIXTIES POLITICS

Britain's first communist peer, Lord Milford, took his seat in the House of Lords in May 1963.

The first female Parliamentary Whip was Harriet Slater (Commons) in October 1964.

The first female Scottish National MP to be elected to Westminster was Winifred Ewing who won the 1967 by-election at Hamilton.

The first black life peer in Britain was Sir Learie Constantine in 1969. He had already achieved fame, and popularity, for his contribution to West Indies cricket and for his campaigning for racial equality, having been knighted in 1962.

Changes were not only abundant in the UK. In Sri Lanka, for instance, Sirimavo Bandaranaike became the world's first female Prime Minister in 1960 – following the assassination of her husband by a monk. In India, Indira Gandhi became that country's first female PM in 1966. She was also a widow – but no relation to Mohandas K. Gandhi. Gandhi is a common name in India, it means 'grocer' or 'seller of perfumes'. In Israel, too, Golda Meir came out of retirement aged 70 to be their first female PM in March 1969, becoming known as the Iron Lady long before Margaret Thatcher was so nicknamed.

POLITICAL NAMES IN THE NEWS

American President, John F. Kennedy, visited Berlin in June 1963 – two years after the wall went up dividing the city (and the world) into capitalists and communists – and made his famous speech about freedom, including the phrase 'Ich bin ein Berliner'.

On his way to Oslo to collect the Nobel Peace Prize in 1964, Martin Luther King stopped off at St Paul's Cathedral in London and presented his sermon – regarding, naturally, racial tensions – on 6 December in front of a full 'house'. (Note that this pre-empted Enoch Powell's notorious 'rivers of blood' speech, attacking British immigration policies, which was not until April 1968.)

When Winston Churchill, the 'last Lion of British politics', died on 24 January 1965, aged 90, it was exactly 70 years (to the day) after the death of his father, Lord Randolph Churchill. His was the first lying-in-state accorded to a non-royal since 1914.

The head of Harold Wilson went missing in 1965 – from Madame Tussaud's. It was returned to police a few days later by the organisers of the Manchester University Students' Rag Week.

In 1966, Chairman Mao Tse Tung (or Zedung) reputedly set a record when he swam 10 miles of China's Yangtze River in under an hour, becoming the first septuagenarian to claim a world swimming record (assisted by a strong current perhaps? Or merely political theatre?). The publicity it generated silenced – temporarily – critics of his ability and his fitness.

After Richard Nixon had a close call to take the US Presidency title (in November 1968), he was in the news again visiting Harold Wilson at Chequers and at 10 Downing Street (February 1969). While in London he stayed at Claridges (of course) and used the imported bullet-proof car provided for him. He also (again of course) met Queen Elizabeth II and the royal family at Buckingham Palace but, less predictably, returned in August to visit RAF Mildenhall in Suffolk. He succeeded Lyndon B. Johnson who had been in the post since 1963, but had not run for re-election. Interestingly, Lyndon B. Johnson is the only US President the queen has not met since her coronation – although he did visit London with his wife in 1960 when he was vice-president. During Johnson's presidency, he made only one visit to Europe and this was an overnight visit to Germany for Konrad Adenauer's funeral in April 1967.

Charles de Gaulle resigned as the French President in 1969 following his defeat in a referendum (not to mention several assassination attempts, left-wing student riots, and a two-week national strike in their support) after constantly denying Britain entrance to the EEC.

LIFE WITH THE ROYALS

The family name was changed in 1960 to Mountbatten-Windsor from what could have been Schleswig-Holstein-Sonderborg-Glucksburg (Prince Philip's family name, or, rather, the name of his derivative royal 'house').

When Princess Margaret married photographer Antony Armstrong-Jones in May 1960, she was the first royal to marry a commoner for 450 years. Not only did the wedding attract the biggest crowds in the street since the queen's coronation, but it was the first to be televised. The Poltimore Tiara she wore (purchased pre-wedding for some £5,000 – which could buy you a house in 1960) had even more press coverage than the simple silk wedding dress, designed by Norman Hartnell.

This was not the only royal wedding in the '60s: Prince Edward, Duke of Kent, married Katharine Worsley in 1961 at York Minster, the first such wedding to take place there for over 600 years. Princess

Alexandra married the Hon. Angus Ogilvy (a City of London banker) two years later at Westminster Abbey, he declining the queen's offer of an earldom to mark the occasion. Overseas weddings included Princess Sophia of Greece to Don Juan Carlos of Spain in 1962 (with Princess Alexandra one of the bridesmaids), and King Constantine of the Hellenes married 18-year-old Princess Anne-Marie of Denmark in 1964. Less predictably, King Hussein of Jordan met (on the set of *Lawrence of Arabia*) and married a telephonist/secretary from Stratford-upon-Avon in 1961, humble Toni Gardiner becoming Princess Muna al Hussein.

Buckingham Palace opened its gates to the paying public for the first time in July 1962, with queues forming to view the Queen's Gallery at a charge of just 2*s* 6*d*. The gallery used the site of the bomb-damaged private chapel.

In 1963, when the queen was expecting Prince Edward, she did not put in an appearance at the opening of Parliament (the only other time was in 1959 when she was expecting Prince Andrew), and she reverted to radio for her Christmas message which had already become established on television. The following year, she had the novel experience (for her) of opening Parliament with a Labour Government, the start of a partnership which crossed the class divide.

In July 1965, the queen made her first visit to the Isle of Wight, which incorporated her first trip on a hovercraft. During the stay, Earl Mountbatten was installed as Governor and Captain of 'all our Isle of Wight'.

When Prince Philip visited Argentina during their 150th independence anniversary celebrations in September/October 1966, shots were fired at the British Embassy where he was staying. Not very friendly.

HRH Edward, Duke of Windsor (ex-King Edward VIII) and his wife, Wallis, Duchess of Simpson, met the queen for the first time since his abdication when they were invited to Marlborough House in London in 1967 for the unveiling of a plaque on the centenary of the birth of his mother, Queen Mary (the queen's grandmother). He sported the Windsor knot tie, naturally. Incidentally, he had stayed in the London Clinic in 1965 for eye surgery, and his wife had also stayed there in 1964 for 'facial surgery' – could explain her youthful looks.

Princess Anne's first public engagement alone and unhindered was to present leeks to the Welsh Guards during a St David's Day ceremony at Pirbright Camp, Surrey, in 1969. And why not?

Prince Charles spent a term at the University College of Wales – learning Welsh – to prepare for his official investiture as Prince of Wales on 1 July 1969 at Caernarvon Castle. The day before the investiture, the first television film about the royal family was shown on television – called, er, *Royal Family*, it was watched by 23 million.

The mother of Prince Philip, Princess Andrew of Greece, died at Buckingham Palace in December 1969. This rather mysterious figure, born deaf, started life as Princess Victoria Alice Elisabeth Julie Marie of Battenberg in Windsor Castle in the presence of Queen Victoria – and is alleged to have given away everything she owned before her demise. She was honoured posthumously by Israel for sheltering Jewish families in Greece during the Second World War.

When the queen decided not to broadcast her annual Christmas message in 1969 because of the amount of exposure the family had had that year, Mary Whitehouse, General Secretary of the National Viewers' and Listeners' Association, handed in 20,000 signatures to Buckingham Palace in protest. It assured a return of the message the following year.

NEW ROYALS INCLUDED . . .

Prince Andrew in 1960, the first birth to a reigning monarch since 1857.

Viscount Linley, Princess Margaret's son, born November 1961.

Lady Sarah Armstrong-Jones, Princess Margaret's daughter, born May 1964.

Prince Edward, youngest son of the queen, born in March 1964.

George, son of the Duchess of Kent, born 1962.

James Ogilvy born February 1964.

Lady Helen Windsor, daughter of the Duchess of Kent, born April 1964.

Princess Alexandra's daughter Marina born 1966.

. . . and not forgetting Lady Diana Spencer, royal-to-be, born in July 1961.

Plus the 9th Earl of Buckinghamshire, Vere Frederick Cecil Hobart-Hampden, who inherited his title from a distant cousin in 1963 while working as a gardener in Southend-on-Sea and living in a council flat. According to reporter Roy Stockdill, Fred the gardener became the 'most assiduous attender' at the Lords, having upped his income from £9 per week to £20 per day for merely turning up at the House of Lords with the cost of a first-class return rail ticket also included. He needed the money as the title was just that, only a title.

Even the royals are not completely free of scandal. In 1963, it was the Duke of Argyll, or, rather, Margaret, the Duchess of Argyll, who was making headlines. This was the summation of their protracted divorce proceedings, when the duke had named 88 of his wife's lovers, but the judge, Lord Wheatley, had decided that three were more than enough – especially with the additional evidence of the salacious photographs of a naked duchess wearing no more than her pearls. It seems that an even bigger calamity for the duke was being asked to resign from his club, a disaster for any 'gentleman'.

THE AGE OF PROTEST AND WAR

The anti-bomb Aldermaston March organised by CND was an annual event at Easter until 1963, with walkers numbering between 30,000 and 100,000, and sales of duffel coats booming. One report of the 1960 march refers to 30 tons of food and 80,000 cups of tea being consumed en route to London. Marches ended in 1963 because of an international treaty which – partially – banned nuclear testing.

In 1960, Harold Macmillan, the then Prime Minister, spoke of a 'wind of change' blowing through Africa – but in fact the whole world was involved in freeing nations to govern themselves. In 1961, South Africa left the Commonwealth and became a republic, a year after the Sharpeville Massacre when police fired on an anti-apartheid demonstration (resulting in the deaths of 56 Africans, but not ending apartheid). But thirty-two other African nations became independent during the decade, from Chad to Rwanda, and from Gambia to Nigeria, which began a different kind of fight in 1967 – this time a Civil War against Biafra. Algeria also gained independence – from France in 1962 following yet another war, which lasted eight years. Celebrations – and new postage stamps – were seen in other countries, e.g. Cyprus (1960), Jamaica (1962), Malta (1964), Singapore (1965), and Southern Yemen (1967) where a military band played 'Fings Ain't What They Used To Be' on the departure of the last British governor after nearly 130 years of British rule.

Although it was the attack on the destroyer USS *Maddox* (by North Vietnam) in August 1964 that brought the US into the Vietnam War officially, a number of Americans had already been killed in the preceding years of conflict. The first American soldier to die in Vietnam in the '60s was in December 1961 – James Davis. Anti-Vietnam war demonstrations in the '60s were the largest ever seen – in the US millions took part in organised rallies and marches in 1969 (250,000 in Washington alone), a year after 80,000 had demonstrated in Trafalgar Square.

In contrast to the protracted Vietnam War, the Arab-Israeli war in 1967 lasted six days: from 4–10 June.

America had further problems in Cuba – where Soviet nuclear missiles were being constructed – until Khruschev agreed to return the missiles to the Soviet Union in October 1962. The latter event (part of the ongoing Cold War between East and West) inspired Dylan's 'A Hard Rain's Gonna Fall' with its reference to the 'roar of a wave that could drown the whole world', i.e. the threat of nuclear war.

The first British troops entered Northern Ireland in August 1969 to quell riots on the streets between the Catholics and Protestants. It seemed like a good idea at the time.

MONEY, MONEY, MONEY

There were a number of changes to the money in your pocket before decimalisation began its gradual introduction in 1968. Black and white £5 notes and the humble farthing (a quarter of an old penny) ceased to be legal tender from 1961. The sixpence, or tanner, was last minted in 1967, despite a 'save our sixpence' campaign, as was the half-crown (2*s* 6*d*), and the halfpenny was withdrawn from circulation in 1969. New £5 notes showing Britannia without her helmet were issued in February 1963, and the first decimal coins (in April 1968, three years before full decimalisation) were the 5p and the 10p, with the 50p coin introduced in October 1969 to replace the old 10*s* note.

Viv and Keith Nicholson (factory worker and miner respectively) won the equivalent of well over £3,000,000 on the football pools in 1961, and Viv became famous for her declaration that she intended to 'Spend, spend, spend!' And spend she did: pink Chevrolet, Harrods gold watch, racehorse . . . By 1965, Keith had been killed in a car accident and Viv was declared bankrupt. Spent, spent, spent.

Top Premium Bond prizes (introduced in the 1950s) were gradually increased in the 1960s – to £5,000 in 1960 (from £1,000), and then to £25,000 in February 1966, the latter in spite of objections from such as politician Norman St John-Stevas who complained that this was effectively encouraging gambling 'when we are facing a very grave gambling problem throughout the country'.

Bookmakers William Hill paid out over £100,000 in July 1969 to punters who had bet that man would walk on the moon before 1970. David Threlfall had put his £10 bet on in 1964 when few believed the feat was possible, and, at 1,000-1, collected more than enough to spend on a very special sports car. A more modest win by a Scottish scientist earned him £1,200 but this paid half the cost of a house he wanted to buy.

Banks, as always, appeared in the news sporadically. The first computer centre for banking opened at Barclays in Drummond Street, London, in 1961. The National Provincial Bank (merged with Nat West in 1968 to become Britain's largest bank) came up with the first cheque guarantee card in 1966, the same year that Barclaycard (the first British credit card) was introduced. Barclays introduced the first cash dispenser card in 1967.

A cool million in 1968 would have bought you . . . London Bridge. This was the price paid by American Robert McCulloch (the chainsaw millionaire) in California for the bridge which was re-erected stone by stone in Lake Havasu City. A 10,000-mile trip and over 10,000 pieces to assemble on arrival. To avoid taxes, the bridge was declared an antique – well, it was well over a hundred years old!

SEVEN NEWSWORTHY ANIMAL STORIES OF THE SIXTIES

Goldie the eagle escaped from Regents Park Zoo in London not once but twice in 1965. In February, he brought London to a stand-still, with as many as 5,000 spectators turning up on a single day to catch a glimpse of the eagle enjoying his freedom in the park's environs. An array of attempts to trap the eagle failed – including an Ethiopian bird pipe, which did not live up to its reputation. Finally tempted down after fifteen days by the prospect of food (well, a dead rabbit) he nipped out of an open cage door again in December – but the bait ploy worked more quickly this time, as he was caught in just a matter of days.

Although there have been previous, and later, sightings of unidentified cat-like beasts, the years between 1964 and 1966 resulted in record-breaking numbers of reports prompting speculation of the existence of the Surrey puma – 362 reports were received by police in Godalming for starters. The closest positive identification followed a sighting at a racing stables near Godalming (September 1966) when a cast of a paw print was taken by the police to London Zoo, who confirmed that it was a puma, but larger than any they had experienced.

The International Whaling Commission placed a worldwide ban on hunting blue whales in 1966 after their numbers had fallen from over 200,000 in pre-whaling days to less than 2,000.

The canine spaceflight record was established in 1966 by Ugolek and Veterok in Kosmos 110. They managed twenty-two days in orbit.

Between 1966 and 1969 several attempts were made to mate giant pandas Chi Chi (London Zoo's lady) with An An (Moscow Zoo's stud), with no success. They tried flying Chi Chi out to Moscow but she got a cold response from An An, and when An An came to London, the Cold War continued. Note that The World Wildlife Fund started life in 1961, founded by Sir Peter Scott using a giant panda as its logo, when Chi Chi was already a popular attraction at London Zoo.

Longleat Safari Park opened its doors in April 1966 as the first drive-through safari park outside Africa. Local Wiltshire inhabitants were not too happy at the prospect of lions roaming the countryside . . . perhaps the idea of the animals being 'free' and the humans being 'caged' (in their cars) was also a bit of a worry.

In 1967, two penguins from Chessington Zoo were taken to Silver Blades ice rink in Streatham, London, to cool off during the August heatwave.

Another lion story, this one about a cub called Christian, who was sold by Harrods in 1969 to owners of a furniture store in King's Road. They kept him in the store until he had to be released into the wilds of Kenya. Nice sales gimmick.

Of the Crufts Best in Show winners in the 1960s, only the German Shepherd and the Lakeland Terrier managed two wins. The name of the 1969 winner (one of the German Shepherds) is particularly memorable: Hendrawen's Nibelung of Charavigne. On second thoughts, his alter ego, Percy, is probably easier to remember.

SOME SIXTIES STATISTICS

66,000 people arrived from the West Indies in 1961 (compared to 1,000 in 1952), and 48,000 from India and Pakistan.

By 1969, the divorce rate was around 51,000 a year, double that of 1959.

The winter of 1962/3 was the worst since 1947, with the coldest January and February since 1740 in Britain. The worst smog for ten years resulted in sixty deaths in December, with a further 800 people admitted to hospital. In some metropolitan areas, visibility was down to nil, and Heathrow Airport was closed for four days – but at least with good reason.

By 1964, half a million British females were taking the revolutionary contraceptive pill. Mothercare, who had opened their first shop only three years earlier, may have been worried.

During the decade, London alone lost 360,000 jobs in manufacturing, including 5,500 when the AEI factory (Associated Electrical Industries) at Woolwich closed in 1968.

UNKNOWNS MAKING NEWS

When Rosemarie Frankland became the first UK winner of the annual Miss World contest in 1961, she was, at the time, the youngest winner at just 18. For those who like statistics (of varying kinds), the girl from Marks and Spencer stood 5ft 6in, 36-22-36 and weighed 8st 12lb.

It transpired that Rosemarie (who was said to have been Bob Hope's on/off mistress for twenty years) was the first of a trio of Miss Worlds from the UK in the 1960s. She was followed by Ann Sidney in 1964 (who had some subsequent success as an actress) and Lesley Langley in 1965 (who secured a role in *Goldfinger*). Coincidentally, Ann and Lesley were both from Dorset – Poole and Weymouth respectively.

Gladys Elton never made it to the big screen but in September 1960, at the age of 81, she performed a strip-tease at the Haslemere Home for the Elderly in Great Yarmouth, an innovative form of entertainment for her peer group. Unfortunately, a male inmate died of a heart attack, and five others were treated for shock. When 87-year-old Harry Meadows dressed up as the Grim Reaper 'for a joke' not many months later, peering through the windows of the very same home, three more of its residents died. But they meant well.

When Christine McDonnell from Dublin entered the record books in 1960, following the birth of her second set of twins on successive leap years (i.e. on 29 February 1960), her only complaint was that she had not put a bet on the event. She would have made a fortune.

A bachelor fishmonger from Wakefield made it into the news in December 1964. Wally Gant became a best man for the 50th time, and saw his name in the *Guinness Book of Records* as well as the local papers.

Rose Boland became headline news in June 1968 as the leading shop steward representing the sewing machinists working at Ford's in Dagenham. In June, these determined ladies went on strike for three weeks in protest at their lack of recognition, and their need to be regraded alongside male staff. They brought Ford's motor production to a standstill, but once Employment Minister Barbara Castle stepped in, they managed to negotiate (almost) all of their aims. Women's trade union membership soared, and equal rights for women were on their way.

Other firsts of a very different kind were Britain's first black headmaster (Tony O'Connor, Warley School, Worcestershire) in 1967 and the first British sextuplets born alive in 1968 to Sheila Thorns in Birmingham at odds of one in three million.

TWENTY CELEBRITY WEDDINGS

1961 Petula Clark and Parisian publicist Claude Wolff in June.
Laurence Olivier and actress Joan Plowright in March, with Richard Burton the best man.

1962 John Lennon and Cynthia Powell in August.

1964 Peter Sellers and actress Britt Ekland in February.
Richard Burton and Elizabeth Taylor – for the first time – in March.
Charlie Watts (the Rolling Stones) and sculptress Shirley Anne Shephard, in October.

1965 Ringo Starr and Maureen Cox, an 18-year-old Liverpool hairdresser (February).

1966 George Harrison and Pattie Boyd in January.
The Who's Keith Moon and 17-year-old Kim Kerrigan (from Sweden) in March. They lived next door to fellow hell-raiser, Oliver Reed.

1967 Elvis Presley and Priscilla Beaulieu in May.
Ian Dury (The Blockheads) and Betty Rathmell in June.
Eric Burdon (The Animals) and model Angela King, in September.

1968 Sandie Shaw and Jeff Banks, the fashion designer, in March.
Jackie Kennedy and Aristotle Onassis in October.
Peter Noone (Herman's Hermits) and Mireille Strasser (French) in November, the day he was issued with a summons by the police for an alleged currency offence.

1969 Cilla Black and her manager Bobby Willis in January.
Lulu and Maurice Gibb (The Bee Gees) in February.
Paul McCartney and Linda Eastman in March, with George Harrison and Pattie Boyd arriving late due to a drug bust.
John Lennon and Yoko Ono also in March (followed by their famous honeymoon in bed in the Amsterdam Hilton).
Billy Fury and model Judith Hall in May.

TOUCHING ON TRAGEDY

Not something to be trivialised, but not something to be ignored, so bearing in mind that the '60s was not just 'peace and love', sex, drugs and rock 'n' roll . . .

The entire (*c.* 300) population of Tristan da Cunha was evacuated to Britain in 1961 following a volcanic eruption. Most of them stayed here for two years, returning when the island was declared safe in 1963.

A small Welsh mining community was devastated by a coal slide in October 1966 which buried the village school, killing 116 children and 28 adults. What became known as the Aberfan Disaster occurred on the last day of term, when the children were singing 'All Things Bright and Beautiful'. Coal had become not just the village livelihood but also the cause of so many deaths.

When the *Torrey Canyon* broke in two in March 1967 after being wrecked between Land's End and the Isle of Scilly, she sent over 100,000 tons of crude oil heading towards Cornwall and the south coast of England. The vessel and the oil had to be literally bombed and covered with napalm but not before over 70 miles of coastline had been polluted. The smoke could be seen 100 miles away, and more marine life was killed and injured by the array of detergents used than by the oil itself. This was regarded as the worst environmental disaster to date, with the Royal Air Force and Royal Navy subject to ridicule because only 10 of the 42 bombs they dropped on the tanker hit the stationary target.

The 1967 outbreak of foot-and-mouth disease was the worst ever seen in Britain – zoos closed, horse racing was cancelled (losing the Government over £1,000,000 a day in lost taxes!), and 134,000 livestock were culled in addition to the hundreds of thousands that died – at a cost of as much as £350,000,000 including millions in compensation for the farmers. Even the Duke of Westminster had to slaughter 60 of his pedigree Dairy Shorthorns. Poor cows.

The collapse of the Ronan Point tower in May 1968 – a 23-storey block of flats in East London – sent out a warning to developers in favour of tower block housing developments. This was not just about the four people killed, but the hundreds effectively 'threatened' with similar disaster.

A FEW FIRSTS AND THE LAST LASTS

The first commemorative British Christmas stamps were issued in December 1966, designed by children who entered a competition run by the GPO. This was also the last year that there was a postal delivery on Christmas Day in Scotland, six years after the service had been discontinued in England.

The first king-size cigarette (Rex) was launched by Lambert & Butler in February 1960 in Britain. Benson & Hedges (Gold) and Embassy were launched in 1962 and Embassy's filter brand became the No. 1 seller, challenged from 1965 by Player's No. 6 (a smaller brand). Unluckily for them, this was the year that cigarette and tobacco advertising was dropped from British television programming. An interesting rival appeared, very briefly, in 1968. Called Bravo, this was a lettuce-based non-tobacco cigarette. Bravo indeed.

The last call-up cards issued for National Service were in December 1960, with the last 2,000 civilians enlisted. Since 1945, 6,000 had been called up every fortnight. The final National Serviceman left the Army on 7 May 1963 – Private Fred Turner of the Catering Corps.

11

ON THIS DAY

1 January 1964 First edition of *Top of the Pops* aired on the BBC.

2 January 1969 Rupert Murdoch beat off Robert Maxwell to take control of the *News of The World*.

3 January 1967 Jack Ruby, killer of JFK's alleged assassin, died in hospital, avoiding execution in the US.

4 January 1967 Donald Campbell killed on Coniston Water during world speed record attempt.

5 January 1962 First record release attributed to the Beatles (and Tony Sheridan, but not in that order!) – 'My Bonnie'.

6 January 1964 The Rolling Stones appeared at the Harrow Granada on the first of their 1964 tour dates – with The Ronettes.

7 January 1967 First episode of controversial *The Forsyte Saga* on the BBC.

8 January 1965 Adam Faith cancelled concerts in South Africa on being refused permission to perform for multi-racial audiences.

9 January 1965 First episode of BBC's *Not Only But Also* – guest star John Lennon.

10 January 1962 Vanessa Redgrave opened with the RSC at the Aldwych Theatre (London) in *As You Like It*.

11 January 1969 Death of Richmal Crompton, the *Just William* writer.

12 January 1964 The Beatles' second appearance at the London Palladium in three months, co-starring with Alma Cogan, and commanding £1,000 instead of the earlier £250.

13 January 1966 Mick Jagger and his girlfriend Chrissie Shrimpton (sister of Jean) visited Dolly's Nightclub in Jermyn Street, London.

14 January 1963 President De Gaulle said 'Non' to Britain joining the EEC.

15 January 1968 The Great Glasgow Storm, killing twenty, and damaging over 70,000 houses (mostly tenements) in the town, as well as unprecedented damage to other areas of western Scotland.

16 January 1961 The first performance of *Orpheus* at the Royal Opera House, Covent Garden (featuring the Covent Garden Opera Ballet), was not well received and was plagued with bad luck: both the designer and principal singer died within months.

17 January 1963 Artist Robert Filliou announced that 'Art' was 1,000,000 years old on this day.

18 January 1963 Leader of the Labour Party, Hugh Gaitskell, died – he was replaced by Harold Wilson.

19 January 1966 Indira Gandhi became India's first woman Prime Minister.

20 January 1964 The start of the trial of the Great Train Robbers.

21 January 1966 George Harrison married Pattie Boyd.

22 January 1963 The Beatles recorded three radio shows in one day: *Saturday Club*, *Pop Inn*, and *The Talent Spot*.

23 January 1960 First edition of *Marty*, the teenage comic named after Marty Wilde.

24 January 1965 Death of Winston Churchill.

25 January 1968 Great Train Robber Charlie Wilson recaptured in Canada four years after escaping from Winson Green Prison in Birmingham.

26 January 1968 Westminster and National Provincial Banks announce they are merging to form Nat West, Britain's largest bank.

27 January 1969 Three astronauts died in Apollo 1 during rehearsals for moon landings.

28 January 1966 The Small Faces released their third single, and biggest success to date, 'Sha-La-La-Lee', which reached No. 3.

29 January 1964 Ninth Winter Olympics opened, at Innsbrück, Austria.

30 January 1965 State funeral of Sir Winston Churchill at St Paul's Cathedral.

31 January 1961 Ham became the first chimpanzee launched into space by the Americans.

1 February 1965 Prescription charges abolished by the Labour Government.

2 February 1961 Len Fairclough (aka actor Peter Adamson) arrived in *Coronation Street.*

3 February 1967 Joe Meek, record producer, killed himself after murdering his landlady on the eighth anniversary of the death of Buddy Holly, one of several dead rock stars he obsessed about.

4 February 1962 First edition of the *Sunday Times c*olour supplement.

5 February 1967 The Rolling Stones appeared on *The Eamonn Andrews Show.*

6 February 1965 Stanley Matthews played his last football match for Stoke – aged 50.

7 February 1964 The Beatles were mobbed at John F. Kennedy Airport when they arrived in the USA for their first visit.

8 February 1966 Laker Airways founded.

9 February 1961 The Beatles' first gig at The Cavern in Liverpool, for a fee of £5.

10 February 1962 Gary Powers, the American U-2 Spy pilot who had been shot down and captured in Russia, was exchanged for the KGB's Colonel Rudolf Abel.

11 February 1965 Ringo Starr married 18-year-old hairdresser Maureen Cox at Caxton Hall in London.

12 February 1968 The Anti-University opened in the City of London.

13 February 1960 The French tested their first nuclear bomb, four times more powerful than Hiroshima, in the French Sahara.

14 February 1963 Harold Wilson became leader of the Labour Party, following the death of Hugh Gaitskell.

15 February 1969 The first human egg was fertilised in a test tube by Robert Edwards in Cambridge.

16 February 1965 Rolling Stones performed in Singapore, the last day of their Far East Tour.

17 February 1962 James Hanratty, the A6 murderer, was found guilty and sentenced to death.

18 February 1969 Lulu (20) married The Bee Gees' Maurice Gibb (19) in a Buckinghamshire church.

19 February 1960 Prince Andrew was born.

20 February 1962 John Glenn became the first American astronaut to orbit the Earth.

21 February 1963 The first £5 note to feature the queen was introduced.

22 February 1968 Release of Genesis' debut single, 'Silent Sun', produced by Jonathan King, the singer/songwriter, but not one of his successes.

23 February 1965 Death of comedic actor Stan Laurel, the British half of Laurel and Hardy.

24 February 1966 Military coup in Ghana resulted in the first president, Kwame Nkrumah, being deposed.

25 February 1964 Cassius Clay beat hot favourite Sonny Liston to take his first world heavyweight title.

26 February 1960 Announcement of the engagement of Princess Margaret to photographer Antony Armstrong-Jones, a romance kept secret from the press.

27 February 1965 Goldie the eagle escaped from London Zoo.

28 February 1966 The Cavern Club, Liverpool, went into liquidation.

1 March 1968 Ringo Starr and his wife Maureen left India after only two weeks – he didn't like the food, and she didn't like the flies.

2 March 1969 Successful test (maiden) flight of Concorde prototype, from Toulouse.

3 March 1969 Launch of Apollo 9 (which featured first Apollo space walk).

4 March 1969 The Kray Twins found guilty of murder at the Old Bailey.

5 March 1963 Hula Hoop patented (in the US).

6 March 1961 The first mini-cabs (Carline Cabs) arrived in London to compete with the traditional black taxi cab.

7 March 1969 The Victoria Line (part of London Underground) was opened by the queen.

8 March 1966 George Cornell shot by Ronnie Kray in the Blind Beggar pub in Whitechapel.

9 March 1967 Joseph Stalin's daughter, Svetlana, defects to the West.

10 March 1964 Prince Edward was born.

11 March 1969 British science-fiction writer, John Wyndham, died.

12 March 1969 Paul McCartney married photographer Linda Eastman (in London).

13 March 1964 Legendary live music club, the Marquee, moved from Oxford Street, London, to larger premises in a disused warehouse in Wardour Street.

14 March 1961 A new New Testament (first part of the New English Bible) was published, and sold four million copies in its first year.

15 March 1968 Foreign Secretary, George Brown, resigned after a row with Harold Wilson.

16 March 1968 Vietnam's My Lai Massacre, with 500 civilians killed – a turning point in the public perception of the war.

17 March 1969 Israel's first woman Prime Minister, Golda Meir, came to power.

18 March 1967 The *Torrey Canyon* was wrecked between Land's End and the Isle of Scilly, sending a huge oil slick towards the coast.

19 March 1963 Acclaimed satire, *Oh! What a Lovely War*, opened at the Theatre Royal, Stratford, East London.

20 March 1969 John Lennon married Yoko Ono, in Gibraltar.

21 March 1963 Alcatraz prison in San Francisco Bay closed due to high costs and security issues.

22 March 1963 John Profumo denied, in the House of Commons, any 'impropriety' in his relationship with Christine Keeler.

23 March 1964 *In His Own Write*, by John Lennon, published.

24 March 1964 The Astoria cinema, in Charing Cross Road, London, hosted the world premier of *The Fall of the Roman Empire*, with full-on Roman décor.

25 March 1961 The final test flight of the Vostok capsule (Sputnik) was sent into orbit by the Russians, complete with Zvezdochka the dog.

26 March 1967 The Dave Clark Five appeared on *The Ed Sullivan Show* for the thirteenth time.

27 March 1968 Yuri Gagarin (the first man to orbit the earth) died in a plane crash in Russia.

28 March 1963 The Shadows instrumental 'Foot Tapper' was top of the charts.

29 March 1964 Radio Caroline, the first pirate station, began broadcasting.

30 March 1964 Clashes between Mods and Rockers at Clacton and elsewhere.

31 March 1966 General election was held – won by Labour with the second largest majority in its history.

1 April 1969 The Hawker-Siddeley 'jump jet' entered the service of the RAF (first aircraft with vertical take-off and landing).

2 April 1962 The first push-button Panda crossing became operational near Waterloo station in London, confusing both drivers and pedestrians.

3 April 1969 John Lennon and Yoko Ono appeared on the *Eamonn Andrews Show* to publicise their peace campaigns – mainly undertaken from their bed.

4 April 1968 Assassination (in Memphis) of Martin Luther King, the civil rights campaigner.

5 April 1962 The Beatles put on a performance for their fan club at the Cavern prior to their departure for Germany. Ticket price was 6*s* 6*d*.

6 April 1965 Capital Gains Tax was introduced in Britain.

7 April 1968 British world racing champion, Jim Clark, was killed at Hockenheim, Germany.

8 April 1963 Julian Lennon (son of) was born, in Liverpool.

9 April 1966 In France, Sophia Loren remarried Carlo Ponti, following the annulment of their first marriage.

10 April 1962 Early Beatle, Stuart Sutcliffe, died in Hamburg, Germany.

11 April 1967 The first professional production of Tom Stoppard's *Rosenkrantz and Guildenstern are Dead* took place at the Old Vic.

12 April 1961 Russian Yuri Gagarin became the first man in space – for 108 minutes, orbiting the earth.

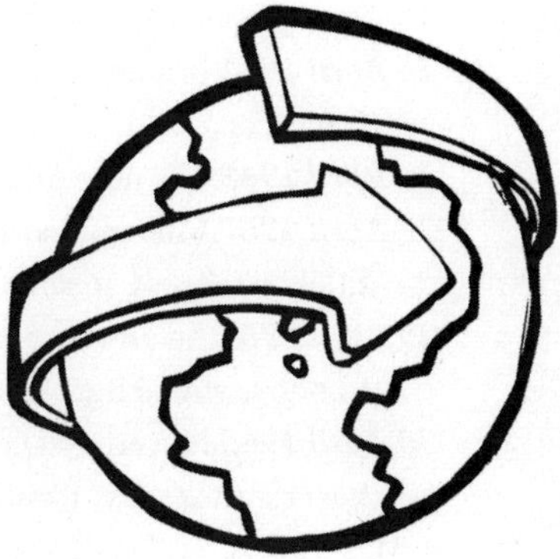

13 April 1964 Sidney Poitier became the first black actor to win an Oscar: for his performance in *Lilies of the Field.*

14 April 1966 The Sussex Downs were recognised as an area of outstanding natural beauty.

15 April 1966 *Time* magazine declared London the City of the decade, the swinging city.

16 April 1969 Desmond Dekker became the first Jamaican musician to top the charts, with 'Israelites'.

17 April 1960 21-year-old rock 'n' roller Eddie Cochran was killed in a car crash in Chippenham, Wiltshire.

18 April 1968 American tycoon Robert McCulloch bought London Bridge for over $2,000,000. He denied mistaking it for Tower Bridge.

19 April 1966 Start of trial of Myra Hindley and Ian Brady for the Moors Murders.

20 April 1968 MP Enoch Powell gave his 'Rivers of Blood' speech, against the Race Relations Bill – and was sacked as a result.

21 April 1964 BBC2 began broadcasting, a day later than planned because of a power blackout.

22 April 1969 British sailor Robin Knox-Johnston became the first yachtsman to sail solo, non-stop, around the world – in 312 days.

23 April 1962 Biggest ever Ban-the-Bomb march ended in a rally of some 150,000 in Hyde Park, London.

24 April 1963 Princess Alexandra married the Hon. Angus Ogilvy at Westminster Abbey.

25 April 1969 Last episode of *The Dales*, the radio programme (previously *Mrs Dale's Diary*) that had been running since 1948. The last line was a twist on Mrs Dale's catchphrase: 'I shall always worry about Jim.'

26 April 1962 Britain's first satellite, Ariel 1, was launched from Cape Canaveral.

27 April 1968 The new Abortion Act came into force in Britain.

28 April 1967 Muhammad Ali stripped of his heavyweight boxing title for refusing to enter the Army (citing religious reasons).

29 April 1967 An all-night rave took place at Alexandra Palace, London, with 41 groups taking part.

30 April 1966 Hoverlloyd commenced the first regular cross-Channel hovercraft service, from Ramsgate to Calais.

1 May 1967 Elvis Presley married Priscilla Beaulieu in Las Vegas.

2 May 1969 The *QE2* set off from Southampton to New York on her maiden voyage.

3 May 1968 Britain's first heart transplant took place at Marylebone's National Heart Hospital.

4 May 1968 Mary Hopkin won *Opportunity Knocks* and was promptly signed by Paul McCartney for Apple Records.

5 May 1961 Alan Shepard became the first American in space – for 15 minutes.

6 May 1960 Princess Margaret married 'commoner' Antony Armstrong-Jones, the photographer, in Westminster Abbey.

7 May 1966 Myra Hindley and Ian Brady began life sentences for the Moors Murders.

8 May 1962 The last trolleybus ran in London.

9 May 1962 The Beatles landed their first recording contract with Parlophone.

10 May 1961 Edwin Bush found guilty of murder – the first in this country to be convicted thanks to the Identikit.

11 May 1964 The first Habitat store was opened in Fulham Road by Terence Conran.

12 May 1969 The minimum voting age in Britain was lowered from 21 to 18.

13 May 1968 A general strike was called in Paris to support rioting students, resulting in a march of 800,000 people seeking Charles de Gaulle's resignation. It nearly brought France to a standstill.

14 May 1967 The ultra-modern Liverpool Catholic Cathedral was consecrated, and promptly rechristened the Mersey Funnel.

15 May 1967 Paul McCartney met Linda Eastman at the Bag O'Nails in London's West End (Kingly Street), where Georgie Fame was playing.

16 May 1968 Ronan Point collapsed in East London, killing four people, and resulting in an anti-tower-block outcry.

17 May 1969 Tom 'Moby' McClean, ex-SAS, became first person to row the Atlantic from west to east (Newfoundland to Ireland).

18 May 1960 The European Cup final was held in Britain for the first time – at Hampden Park, Glasgow. The result was a 7–3 win for Real Madrid over Eintracht Frankfurt.

19 May 1966 The Post Office Tower's restaurant and viewing galleries in London were opened to the public.

20 May 1962 Bobby Moore's first appearance for England – in the World Cup, with a 4–0 victory against Peru.

21 May 1966 Cassius Clay knocked out Henry Cooper to retain his world heavyweight title at the Arsenal football ground.

22 May 1967 UK launch of *Practical Caravan* magazine.

23 May 1969 Release of *Tommy*, the first rock opera album by The Who.

24 May 1962 Elvis hit No.1. in the UK with 'Good Luck Charm', and hung on for five weeks.

25 May 1961 English typist Toni Gardiner married King Hussein of Jordan, converting to Islam on marriage.

26 May 1969 John Lennon and Yoko Ono start their second bed-in, in Montreal, promoting world peace.

27 May 1961 The first Golden Rose of Montreux Award was won by the BBC for *The Black and White Minstrel Show*.

28 May 1967 Sir Francis Chichester arrived in Plymouth on his yacht, *Gipsy Moth IV*, after his solo 119-day trip around the world – the first to do the trip with just one stop, in Sydney.

29 May 1961 Prince Philip became the first royal to be interviewed on television – by David Dimbleby, for *Panorama*.

30 May 1966 British driver Graham Hill was the first to win the Indianapolis 500 on his debut appearance since 1927.

31 May 1965 Another Brit, Jim Clark, became first non-American for nearly 50 years to win the Indianapolis 500, and the first winner in a rear-engined car.

1 June 1967 Release of The Beatles' *Sergeant Pepper's Lonely Hearts Club Band*.

2 June 1962 Britain's first legal casino opened in the Metropole Hotel, Brighton.

3 June 1964 Rolling Stones began their first US tour, with Bobby Vee.

4 June 1964 Record-breaking Yorkshire cricketer Geoff Boycott debuted for England (v Australia) at Trent Bridge.

5 June 1968 Senator Robert Kennedy was assassinated at the Ambassador Hotel in Los Angeles.

6 June 1966 The controversial sit-com *Till Death Us Do Part* began its first series on the BBC.

7 June 1967 Reggie Kray's wife, Frances, committed suicide.

8 June 1964 Christine Keeler, made famous in the Profumo affair, was released from prison after serving six months of a nine-month sentence for perjury.

9 June 1964 Death of Lord Beaverbrook, MP and press baron.

10 June 1968 Prescription charges reinstated by Labour.

11 June 1965 The Royal Albert Hall (London) hosted the International Poetry Incarnation complete with US beat poets.

12 June 1965 The Beatles awarded – controversially – MBEs.

13 June 1969 20-year-old Mick Taylor (from John Mayall's Bluesbreakers) took Brian Jones' place in The Rolling Stones.

14 June 1964 Nelson Mandela sentenced to life imprisonment on Robben Island.

15 June 1966 Lord Mountbatten, Admiral of the Fleet, opened the world's first 'Hovershow' in Hampshire.

16 June 1967 50,000 attended the Monterey Pop Festival in California, launching the Summer of Love.

17 June 1961 Russian ballet star Rudolf Nureyev defected to the West.

18 June 1963 Henry Cooper came close to knocking out Cassius Clay at Wembley – but Clay was, literally, saved by the bell, and ended up with a controversial victory.

19 June 1967 Paul McCartney appeared on *Independent Television News*, when he admitted to taking LSD.

20 June 1966 Sheila Scott landed at Heathrow after 33 days, having become the first British woman to fly solo around the world.

21 June 1963 Pope Paul VI took office, the last to be regally 'crowned'.

22 June 1969 Iconic star Judy Garland died at 47 of a drug overdose at her Chelsea home, just months after her fifth marriage.

23 June 1967 The Who's John Entwistle (the one who stood stock still!) married his childhood sweetheart, Alison.

24 June 1968 Comedian Tony Hancock committed suicide, age 44, while in Australia.

25 June 1969 The longest-ever (then) singles match took place at Wimbledon between Americans Pancho Gonzales and Charlie Pasarell – 5 hours 12 minutes.

26 June 1963 During Kennedy's visit to Berlin, he famously announced 'Ich bin ein Berliner' [I am a Berliner].

27 June 1967 The first of the high street banks introduced a cash dispensing machine in Enfield, North London, namely Barclays.

28 June 1969 The Stonewall Riots in New York, which saw the birth of the Gay Rights Movement.

29 June 1967 Mick Jagger and Keith Richard sentenced to three and twelve months respectively for possession of illegal substances.

30 June 1960 Hit musical *Oliver!* opened at the New Theatre, St Martin's Lane, London, for the first of over 2,500 performances.

1 July 1967 Colour television began in Britain with Wimbledon coverage on BBC2.

2 July 1965 American macho author, Ernest Hemingway, shot himself.

3 July 1969 Brian Jones of the Rolling Stones was found drowned in his swimming pool.

4 July 1968 Britain's Alec Rose, 59, landed at Portsmouth after sailing round the world solo in 354 days, and received a hero's welcome.

5 July 1969 A free Rolling Stones concert in Hyde Park, London (in memory of Brian Jones) attracted 250,000 people.

6 July 1964 The Beatles' first film, *A Hard Day's Night*, premiered in London with Princess Margaret in attendance.

7 July 1967 Award-winning actress Vivien Leigh died of tuberculosis.

8 July 1961 First all British final in Wimbledon's women's singles since 1914 resulted in a win for Angela Mortimer over favourite Christine Truman.

9 July 1962 The largest man-made nuclear explosion (in outer space) took place from Johnston Island, USA, causing electrical damage in Hawaii, 900 miles away.

10 July 1965 The Rolling Stones reached No. 1. in the US for the first time with 'I Can't Get No Satisfaction'.

11 July 1962 Following the launch of the Telstar communication satellite, the first pictures from the USA 'arrived' in Goonhilly, Cornwall.

12 July 1969 Tony Jacklin became the first Brit for 18 years to win the British Open Golf Championship (at Lytham St Anne's).

13 July 1967 Tom Simpson, the first Brit to win the World Championship Road Race, died of exhaustion during the 13th stage of the Tour de France.

14 July 1966 French star Brigitte Bardot married German playboy Gunter Sachs (her third husband) in Las Vegas.

15 July 1965 Mariner IV sent back the first close-up pictures of another planet – Mars.

16 July 1969 Apollo 11 launched on moon mission.

17 July 1968 The Beatles attended the premiere of *Yellow Submarine* at the London Pavilion.

18 July 1961 First Prime Minister's Question Time, with Harold Macmillan.

19 July 1969 Brit John Fairfax became the first man to row east to west solo across the Atlantic.

20 July 1968 Jane Asher told Simon Dee, on air, that her seven-month engagement to Paul McCartney had ended.

21 July 1969 Neil Armstrong took 'one small step for man' – on the moon.

22 July 1967 David Raven celebrated ten years playing Major Metcalf in *The Mousetrap* – the longest single engagement by any stage actor in one part.

23 July 1965 Saul Hudson, better known as Slash, of Guns n' Roses, was born in London.

24 July 1965 Boxer Freddie Mills found shot dead in his car in Soho.

25 July 1962 The Queen's Gallery (part of the Buckingham Palace complex) was opened to the public for the first time.

26 July 1963 A new national speed limit of 50mph was introduced in the UK for five weekends as a trial.

27 July 1964 Winston Churchill appeared for the last time in the House of Commons.

28 July 1965 President Johnson announced that he was sending 44 more battalions to Vietnam, bringing the US presence to 125,000 men.

29 July 1964 The first Brook Advisory Centre opened in London – a 'sex clinic' for the young.

30 July 1966 Victory for England against West Germany in the World Cup – 4–2 after extra time.

31 July 1965 Advertisements for cigarettes were banned on British television.

1 August 1968 The first hover-ferry service (the *Princess Margaret*, named by HRH the day before) started operating from Dover to Boulogne.

2 August 1964 Mods and Rockers clashed at Hastings.

3 August 1963 Stephen Ward died after a sleeping pill overdose, at the end of his trial for living on immoral earnings, part of the Profumo affair.

4 August 1966 The opening ceremony of the 8th British Empire and Commonwealth Games in Jamaica, the first outside the 'white dominions'.

5 August 1962 Marilyn Monroe found dead, under 'suspicious' circumstances.

6 August 1966 At Earl's Court, Cassius Clay knocked out English heavyweight Brian London in Round 3.

7 August 1965 Mike Smith of the Dave Clark Five was pulled from the stage by an over-enthusiastic fan in Chicago, and ended up with two broken ribs.

8 August 1963 The Great Train Robbery, when the Glasgow–London train was relieved of £2.5 million in used notes in just 42 minutes.

9 August 1963 First showing of ITV's *Ready, Steady, Go!* with Billy Fury and Brian Poole.

10 August 1964 In Liverpool, Mick Jagger was fined (£32) for driving over the speed limit and without insurance.

11 August 1968 The last trip by a mainline steam passenger train ran from Liverpool to Carlisle.

12 August 1964 The death of author Ian Fleming.

13 August 1964 The last executions in Britain – Peter Allen in Liverpool and Gwynne Evans in Manchester.

14 August 1969 The first British troops were deployed in Northern Ireland to restore order.

15 August 1969 The start of the Woodstock Music Festival (New York state), the largest single gathering of people to listen to music, i.e. over half a million.

16 August 1962 The Beatles' original drummer, Pete Best, is sacked by Brian Epstein.

17 August 1960 The Beatles began their first Hamburg club engagement at the Indra.

18 August 1965 Photographer David Bailey married French filmstar Catherine Deneuve in London, with Mick Jagger as best man.

19 August 1960 American pilot Gary Powers found guilty of espionage (in Moscow) and sentenced to ten years.

20 August 1965 Andrew Oldham (The Rolling Stones' manager) launched Immediate Records, with 'Hang On Sloopy' by the McCoys.

21 August 1965 When Keith Peacock was called on to the pitch for Charlton Athletic against Bolton Wanderers, he became the first substitute to play in a football league match.

22 August 1964 The first *Match of the Day* was screened by BBC2.

23 August 1962 John Lennon married his pregnant girlfriend, Cynthia, in Liverpool.

24 August 1968 Yoko Ono and John Lennon appeared in their first television interview together – on *Frost on Saturday*.

25 August 1960 The Olympic Games opened in Rome.

26 August 1967 The Beatles attended a lecture by Maharishi Yogi in Bangor University, just days after meeting him in London; and promptly denounced the use of drugs at the later press conference.

27 August 1967 Brian Epstein (the Beatles' manager) died of a drug overdose, following two earlier suicide attempts.

28 August 1963 Martin Luther King made his 'I have a dream' speech in Washington, in front of 200,000.

29 August 1966 The Beatles played their last live concert – in Candlestick Park, San Francisco. They – especially John – had had 'enough'.

30 August 1960 The border between East and West Berlin was closed – a year before the wall went up.

31 August 1962 Chris Bonington and Ian Clough became the first Brits to conquer the north face of the Eiger.

1 September 1968 The first section of the new Victoria line on London Underground was opened (Walthamstow to Highbury).

2 September 1968 *The Morecambe and Wise Show* began its first series on the BBC.

3 September 1966 Paratroopers Chay Blyth and John Ridgway landed on the Isle of Aran after spending 92 days rowing the Atlantic, the first duo across.

4 September 1965 The Who had their van and instruments stolen while they were buying a guard dog from Battersea Dogs' Home.

5 September 1963 Christine Keeler was arrested and charged with perjury as a result of the Profumo scandal.

6 September 1966 South African Prime Minister Hendrik Verwoerd (supposed architect of apartheid) assassinated in Cape Town.

7 September 1964 The first Biba opened – a small boutique in Abingdon Road, Kensington.

8 September 1968 Brit Virginia Wade beat USA's Billie Jean King to win the first US Open Tennis Championship.

9 September 1969 First edition of *Nationwide* was transmitted by the BBC.

10 September 1964 Rod Stewart recorded his first and only single for Decca – 'Good Morning Little Schoolgirl'. It failed to chart.

11 September 1967 The Beatles' Magical Mystery Tour bus started out from Baker Street in London.

12 September 1960 The first MOT tests were introduced for cars over ten years old.

13 September 1969 The Toronto Rock and Roll Revival music festival featured the first live performance of the Plastic Ono Band.

14 September 1961 The first Mothercare store opened in Kingston-upon-Thames.

15 September 1964 The *Sun* came out today – for the first time.

16 September 1968 The Post Office introduced a two-tier postal system, with 2nd class at 4*d* and 1st at 5*d*.

17 September 1961 London's biggest ever ban-the-bomb demo ended in Trafalgar Square with over 800 arrests including Vanessa Redgrave and George Melly.

18 September 1960 Last day of the Picasso exhibition at the Tate Gallery, London.

19 September 1960 The first traffic wardens appeared in Westminster, London, as a result of the 1960 Road Traffic Act.

20 September 1967 The *QE2* was launched at Clydebank at a cost of £29 million – although its maiden voyage had to wait another 18 months.

21 September 1969 Members of the London Street Commune were evicted from their squat at a 100-room mansion at 144 Piccadilly by 200 police.

22 September 1962 Launch of 'swinging' – but short-lived – teen magazine *Serenade.*

23 September 1961 At Oulton Park track in Cheshire, Stirling Moss won the International Gold Cup – the first F1 win in a 4-wheel-drive.

24 September 1966 Jimi Hendrix set foot on British soil with pink plastic hair curlers and a jar of acne cream in his suitcase.

25 September 1965 A cartoon series featuring animated Beatles launched in the USA and lasted on ABC television until 1969.

26 September 1963 Lord Denning's report on the Profumo affair was published.

27 September 1968 The controversial premiere of *Hair*, in London's West End, hours after the easing of theatre censorship in Britain.

28 September 1964 Death of Adolph 'Harpo' Marx – the 'mute' one.

29 September 1967 The last day for BBC Radio's Light Programme, Third Programme and Home Service.

30 September 1967 Tony Blackburn kicked off the first Radio One breakfast show with 'Flowers in the Rain' by The Move.

1 October 1966 Jimi Hendrix made his UK stage debut when he jammed with Cream at the Central London Polytechnic, upstaging Eric Clapton.

2 October 1968 The day of the first recorded case of live sextuplets born in Britain to Sheila Thorns from Birmingham.

3 October 1967 The death of Sir Malcolm Sargent, the conductor, in the same week that Stamford (his home ground) was designated Britain's first urban conservation area.

4 October 1965 Paul VI was the first pope to land on US soil when he travelled to New York to address the United Nations.

5 October 1969 The first episode of *Monty Python's Flying Circus* aired on BBC2.

6 October 1968 Jackie Stewart, Graham Hill and John Surtees took the first three places in the US Grand Prix.

7 October 1966 Johnny Kidd was killed in a car crash on the M1, his band (Johnny Kidd and the Pirates – remember 'Shakin' All Over'?) having started out as Freddie Heath and the Nutters.

8 October 1967 The breathalyser was used for the first time in Britain (in Somerset).

9 October 1967 Socialist revolutionary Che Guevara was executed by the Bolivian Army.

10 October 1961 The entire population of Tristan da Cunha in the South Atlantic was evacuated to Britain following a volcanic eruption.

11 October 1963 Gerry Marsden (of Pacemakers fame) married the former secretary of his fan club, Pauline Behan.

12 October 1968 The Olympic Games opened in Mexico City and, for the first time, winners had to have drug tests.

13 October 1963 The Beatles made their first appearance at the London Palladium.

14 October 1969 The 50p coin replaced the 10s note.

15 October 1964 A general election resulted in a narrow majority for Harold Wilson, who became the (then) youngest British Prime Minister of the twentieth century.

16 October 1967 Folk singer Joan Baez was one of those arrested on a day of anti-Vietnam-war protests in the USA.

17 October 1968 At the Mexico Olympics, American medal-winning athletes raised gloved hands in protest at US racial segregation.

18 October 1966 A belated royal pardon was handed out to Timothy Evans, hanged in 1950 for the murder of his wife and child.

19 October 1963 Following the Profumo affair, Sir Alec Douglas-Home took over from Harold Macmillan as the next Conservative PM.

20 October 1960 The court case against Penguin's publication of *Lady Chatterley's Lover* began in London.

21 October 1960 Britain's first nuclear submarine, HMS *Dreadnought*, was launched by the Queen at Barrow-in-Furness.

22 October 1966 Spy George Blake escaped from the maximum security wing of Wormwood Scrubs after serving just four of his 42 years' sentence.

23 October 1966 'Hey Joe' was recorded by the Jimi Hendrix Experience in London – their first single.

24 October 1969 A serious riot resulting in dozens of injuries took place at Parkhurst (on the Isle of Wight) after the early release of Russian spy Peter Kroger.

25 October 1961 *Private Eye*, the popular satirical magazine, first published.

26 October 1965 The Beatles collected their MBEs at Buckingham Palace.

27 October 1967 The Abortion Bill came into force.

28 October 1962 A day of relief around the world when the Cuban Missile Crisis ended, with Russia agreeing to ship their missiles back 'home'.

29 October 1967 Jack 'The Hat' McVitie was murdered by Reggie Kray, although it was two years before he was convicted. (Some sources give 28th, but it is more likely the early hours of the 29th.)

30 October 1967 Brian Jones (The Rolling Stones) was jailed for possessing Indian hemp, but out on bail a day later.

31 October 1964 The Windmill Theatre said goodbye to the Windmill Girls after 32 years.

1 November 1968 George Harrison released the first of the Beatles' solo albums – *Wonderwall* – the first LP from Apple Records.

2 November 1964 The first episode of *Crossroads* was transmitted by ATV, the start of a long run (over twenty years).

3 November 1961 Viscount Linley, son of Princess Margaret and Antony Armstrong-Jones, was born at Clarence House.

4 November 1963 The Beatles famously appeared on the Royal Variety Show, with the Queen Mother in attendance. (Famous? Because John Lennon suggested wealthy patrons 'rattle their jewellery' in lieu of clapping.)

5 November 1968 Richard Nixon was elected the 37th President of the USA.

6 November 1968 Independent airline, British Eagle, ceased trading.

7 November 1967 Henry Cooper beat Billy Walker at Wembley, becoming the first boxer to win three Lonsdale belts.

8 November 1968 Eric Morecambe (of Morecambe and Wise), suffered a massive heart attack while driving to his hotel from the Variety Club in Batley – he had to ask a passing stranger to take him to A&E.

9 November 1960 John Kennedy took on the Presidency of the USA, the first Catholic in the role.

10 November 1969 Gene Autry received a gold record for 'Rudolph The Red-Nosed Reindeer', recorded twenty years earlier.

11 November 1965 Britain's last African colony, Rhodesia, declared an independent state by Ian Smith's government.

12 November 1965 Marc Bolan was on *Ready, Steady, Go!* performing his first single, 'The Wizard'.

13 November 1969 Essex mum Irene Hanson gave birth to Britain's first surviving quintuplets at Queen Charlotte's Hospital, London.

14 November 1969 Apollo 12 took off on the second successful mission to the moon.

15 November 1969 BBC1 and ITV's first colour transmissions.

16 November 1966 The controversial *Cathy Come Home* aired on BBC watched by 12 million.

17 November 1960 The last National Service recruits signed on.

18 November 1963 The first Dartford Tunnel, linking Kent and Essex under the Thames, opened at a cost of £13,000,000.

19 November 1969 *The Benny Hill Show* aired for the first time on Thames Television.

20 November 1961 The new Dungeness Lighthouse, Kent, was opened.

21 November 1969 The short-lived *Curry and Chips* aired on LWT, the first comedy in colour (in various senses).

22 November 1963 President Kennedy was assassinated.

23 November 1963 The BBC premiered *Dr Who*, 'an adventure in space and time', with William Hartnell as the Doctor.

24 November 1963 Lee Harvey Oswald (the supposed assassinator of Kennedy) was shot and killed in Dallas.

25 November 1969 John Lennon returned his MBE as a peace 'protest'.

26 November 1968 The Race Relations Act came into force.

27 November 1969 First of two appearances at New York's Madison Square Garden by the Rolling Stones, billed the rock event of the year, and recorded for posterity as 'Get Yer Ya-Yas Out'.

28 November 1968 Alzheimer's-related death of children's writer Mrs Mary Pollock, better known as Enid Blyton.

29 November 1965 Mary Whitehouse announced the formation of the National Viewers' and Listeners' Association, to operate as the BBC watchdog.

30 November 1968 The Trade Descriptions Act became law.

1 December 1966 The first British commemorative Christmas stamps were issued.

2 December 1965 Tony Hancock married his publicity agent 'Freddie' Ross at Marylebone Register Office in London.

3 December 1967 The first successful human heart transplant was achieved by Dr Christian Barnard in Cape Town, South Africa.

4 December 1961 The British NHS introduced the contraceptive pill thanks to Enoch Powell, Minister of Health.

5 December 1967 A launch party was held for the Apple boutique (Baker Street, London) with John Lennon and George Harrison in attendance – as a boutique, without a drinks licence, the tipple served was . . . apple juice.

6 December 1964 Martin Luther King gave a sermon at St Paul's Cathedral in London.

7 December 1964 Eric Clapton made his first appearance at the Royal Albert Hall, with the Yardbirds.

8 December 1962 The UK's last serious smog (in London) cleared after five days and hundreds of deaths.

9 December 1960 *Coronation Street* aired for the first time.

10 December 1964 British Professor Dorothy Hodgkin received the Nobel Prize for Chemistry, following in Marie Curie's footsteps.

11 December 1967 Around 1,000 spectators had their first view of Concorde when it was unveiled at Toulouse.

12 December 1967 The Stones' Brian Jones won his appeal against his jail sentence for possession of illegal drugs – he was fined (£1,000) and placed on probation instead.

13 December 1965 The first episode of *Jackanory*, which became hugely popular.

14 December 1962 Unmanned US craft Mariner II passed closer to Venus than any previous mission, establishing radio contact which produced what was described as the Music of the Spheres.

15 December 1966 The death of Walt Disney, producing a legend about his body being frozen, but not established in fact.

16 December 1967 The Rolling Stones signed up Marianne Faithfull for their own record label, Mother Earth (although they were still tied into Decca).

17 December 1968 11-year-old Mary Bell sentenced to detention for life for the manslaughter of two young boys.

18 December 1969 Britain formally abolished the death penalty for murder upon the agreement of the House of Commons and the House of Lords.

19 December 1962 The expensively redesigned Empire Theatre in Leicester Square, London, reopened with Doris Day and Jimmy Durante in *Jumbo*.

20 December 1962 *Rule of Three*, Agatha Christie's last West End play, had its first night at the Duchess Theatre.

21 December 1964 Publication of *Ode to a High Flying Bird* (i.e. jazz man Charlie 'Bird' Parker), written by the Stones' drummer, Charlie Watts.

22 December 1965 Britain introduced the 70mph speed limit on motorways.

23 December 1966 The last edition of ITV's *Ready, Steady, Go!*.

24 December 1968 Apollo 8 became the first manned spacecraft to orbit the moon.

25 December 1967 Paul McCartney and Jane Asher announced their engagement.

26 December 1967 First airing of the Beatles' *Magical Mystery Tour* – on the BBC.

27 December 1965 Oil rig Sea Gem collapsed in the North Sea, with a dozen fatalities.

28 December 1963 The last episode of *That Was The Week That Was* (or *TW3*) was shown by the BBC.

29 December 1966 The Jimi Hendrix Experience recorded their debut on *Top of the Pops* performing 'Hey Joe'.

30 December 1969 Former policeman Howard Wilson shot three policemen while trying to resist arrest for a bank robbery in Glasgow (two died, and Wilson was sentenced to life imprisonment).

31 December 1964 Donald Campbell broke the water-speed record on Lake Dumbleyung in Australia.